A Reconstructed Corpse

A Reconstructed Corpse

Simon Brett

VICTOR GOLLANCZ

LONDON

First published in Great Britain 1993
by Victor Gollancz
A Cassell imprint
Villiers House, 41/47 Strand, London WC2N 5JE

A catalogue record for this book is
available from the British Library

ISBN 0 575 05641 X

Photoset in Great Britain by
Rowland Phototypesetting Ltd, Bury St Edmunds, Suffolk
and printed by St Edmundsbury Press Ltd,
Bury St Edmunds, Suffolk

To IAN AND PENNY,

with thanks for the idea

Chapter One

Charles Paris had never thought that he looked like a murder victim. And for most of his life he didn't. But then someone who looked a little like the actor apparently got himself murdered, and Charles Paris was faced with the unusual prospect of employment.

It was for a programme called *Public Enemies*, one of the rash of 'True Crime' series which had suddenly appeared on British television. Like the others in the genre, the hour-long *Public Enemies* programmes used a worthy, pious, together-we-can-beat-crime approach to pander to its audience's worst instincts of prurience and ghoulishness.

The programme was presented with straight-faced grittiness by self-appointed 'man of the people' Bob Garston who, after lucrative excursions into the lighter areas of television game shows, had returned to what he continuously described as his 'no-nonsense hard-bitten journalistic roots'. (Usually he also managed to get a reference to 'working at the coalface of real life' into the same sentence.)

Public Enemies was produced for ITV by West End Television, 'in association with Bob's Your Uncle Productions'. Bob Garston had, in common with many other successful presenters and writers, formed his own production company to secure a bigger slice of profits and greater control over the shows he worked on. The company's name reflected his game-show identity rather than his serious crime-fighter image, but was retained because its on-screen credit had already appeared on a good few programmes. That put 'Bob's Your Uncle' into an exclusive minority, way ahead of the recent proliferation of other

7

independent production companies which had never made a programme.

Charles Paris had worked for WET before, but never through an independent producer, and from his first interview for the job, one morning early in November, he was aware of tensions between Roger Parkes, executive producer for the parent company, and Bob's Your Uncle Productions, represented by Bob Garston himself. The presenter had always regarded shows he worked on as private adventure playgrounds for his ego. The involvement of his own production company seemed to him completely to vindicate this attitude, and justify the inexorable imposition of his will on every aspect of the proceedings.

In common with most megalomaniacs, Bob Garston totally lacked the ability to delegate. His management style depended on personally monitoring all details of the production process. The workload this entailed might from time to time threaten to drive him into the ground, but at least doing everything himself allayed Bob Garston's increasingly paranoid fears that somebody might be doing something behind his back.

So he was present even at the interviews to find an actor who resembled the missing Martin Earnshaw, the kind of chore that most producers would have delegated to a casting director. Because Garston was there, so was Roger Parkes. The executive producer had caught on to the presenter's penchant for making decisions behind his back, and now tried to cover every move.

A casting director was present as well, Dana Wilson, fastidiously groomed and languid to the point of torpor. Letting Bob Garston run all the interviews and make all the decisions perfectly suited Dana's inert approach to her job.

Charles Paris had met the casting director before. He'd had a general interview with her some years earlier. Come to that, he'd met Bob Garston too, worked with him on the pilot of *If the Cap Fits!*, the mindless entertainment whose long run had been the foundation of all the presenter's subsequent game-show successes. But Charles didn't expect either of them to remember him. The peremptory phone call from the programme's researcher Louise Denning announcing the time of his call had reminded him of the low priority held by good manners in television.

He was proved right. Neither his name nor his face produced the tiniest flicker of recognition from Bob Garston or Dana Wilson.

Charles did sometimes wonder whether he actually looked anonymous. He hoped not. Though actors pride themselves on their versatility, they still like to feel they have a core of individualism, which separates them from the other faces that beam – or more frequently these days scowl – from the pages of *Spotlight*.

But Charles's positive sense of his own identity was frequently undermined. Like most actors, he had the knack of remembering none of the good, but all of his bad notices, and one that rankled particularly had come from the *East Kent Mercury*. 'Charles Paris was apparently in the play too, though he made so little impression that it was easy to overlook the fact.' He would have minded less if he hadn't been playing Hamlet.

Nor was his sense of identity much bolstered by his agent. Maurice Skellern, in a rare moment of analysing his client's strengths and weaknesses, had once said, 'Thing about you, Charles, is you're one of those actors who blends in anywhere. You can play anything.'

'Except major parts, it seems,' the actor had responded bitterly.

'But that's your *strength*, Charles. Stars may do very well when they're on top, but when they run out of star parts they're finished. Whereas actors like you *never* need to be out of work.'

'If that's the case, Maurice, why is it that I'm *always* out of work?'

'Ah, well . . .' But the agent was never thrown for long. He

9

always had the same excuse at the ready. 'Thing is, Charles, things are very *quiet* at the moment.'

'Been *quiet* for rather a long time, haven't they?'

'Well, yes . . . that is in the nature of the business, of your chosen profession. And also, Charles . . .' Maurice had paused, trying to shape his next words in the least harmful way possible. 'The fact is you don't always help yourself . . .'

'How do you mean?'

'Well, actors do have to *get out there*, you know. See people . . . hustle a bit . . . *network*, know what I mean . . . ?'

The only response to this had been a grunt.

'Thing is, with the best will in the world, Charles . . .' Why is it that people always start like that when they're about to demonstrate lavish amounts of ill will? 'With the best will in the world, I have to say that you do tend to be rather *passive* in your approach to your career.'

'Well, I'm not sure that I'd say—'

'I mean, I do everything I can, *I work my butt off* on your behalf, but you do have to take the occasional initiative yourself, you know.'

The conversation had left Charles, as all conversations with his agent left him, fuming and furious. For Maurice Skellern, an agent who had raised inactivity to the level of an art form, to claim he 'worked his butt off' on behalf of a client was . . . It made Charles so angry he couldn't finish the thought. And what made him even angrier was the knowledge that there was a lot of truth in what his agent had said.

It actually was through Maurice that he'd been contacted for the *Public Enemies* job. Not that any effort on the agent's part had been required. The programme's researcher Louise Denning had trawled through *Spotlight* looking for faces which resembled the missing – presumed murdered – Martin Earnshaw, had found Charles's in the back section of quarter-page photographs, and simply phoned the agent listed.

No one would have known this, however, from the way Maurice presented the situation to his client. 'You know how I'm always beavering away on your behalf, Charles, never letting any potential opening slip by. Well, some of my groundwork at WET's beginning to pay off. After my relentless bombardment of them with reminders about you, they've finally come back to me with something.'

'What is it?' Charles had asked, as ever unable to flatten out the instinctive surge of excitement any chance of work prompted. *This time*, he always thought, this time maybe it'll happen. This time my talent'll be taken seriously, this time I'll be offered something meaty at the National or a major telly series.

But this time was, as ever, another disappointment. To rub salt in the wound, this time the approach had no connection at all with his acting talent. Charles Paris had been short-listed simply because his face fitted. God, it was so humiliating.

Even so, when he went to the interview, he desperately wanted to get the job.

To call the encounter an 'interview' was over-flattering. It was more like a police line-up, which, given the nature of the programme, was perhaps appropriate.

Five potential Martin Earnshaws had been called, and they were told to parade in front of a screen with height-lines marked on it. Charles found the selection process mystifying. Though a couple of the candidates looked vaguely like each other, none of them seemed to bear the slightest resemblance to him. And since he couldn't see the photographs which Bob Garston, Roger Parkes and Dana Wilson so assiduously pored over, he couldn't judge whether any of them looked at all like the missing Martin Earnshaw.

During the selection no attempt was made to treat the aspirants like human beings. Their physical attributes and oddities were anatomized without restraint. They were there simply as set-dressing and the winner would be the one who most closely fitted the preconceived design.

It turned out to be Charles Paris, though Roger Parkes had favoured one of the other candidates. Still, Bob Garston made the decisions and, with that lack of tact only mastered by the totally self-absorbed, bulldozed the executive producer's opinion out of the way. Bob did not even notice the tight-lipped manner in which Roger Parkes walked out of the room, saying he had 'other things to be getting on with'.

Even when informed that he'd got the job, Charles was still treated as if he wasn't there. This didn't surprise him. He'd worked in television long enough to know what to expect. No one even offered to show him a photograph of the man he apparently so resembled.

The casting decision made, Bob Garston bustled off to lean inhibitingly over the shoulder of some other member of the production team, while Dana Wilson suppressed her yawns long enough to take down Charles's details.

'You should actually have them all on file,' he said.

She looked puzzled. 'Why?'

'Well, I have worked for WET a few times before.'

'Oh really?' This information made not the tiniest dent in the impermeable surface of Dana Wilson's mind. 'Full name . . . ?'

It's strange how some murders are sexy. Not sexy in the sense of being sexually motivated, but sexy in the sense that the media takes them up and keeps on and on about them.

Whether a murder becomes sexy or not depends on the personnel involved. The killing of a pretty woman always attracts the press. Colour photos of her in her prime, snapped laughing in a strapless dress at a disco, can be juxtaposed with bleak shots of the alley or waste ground where she met her end. Newspaper readers enjoy the *frisson* prompted by such contrasts, seeing how quick bright things have come to confusion.

Love triangles also catch the public imagination, regardless of the glamour of the participants. A wife and lover plotting the demise of a husband is a reliable stand-by; while a woman removing her rival for a man's affections is even more popular. When it comes to sexy murders, the public know what they like, and fortunately in this country there are enough people of homicidal tendencies to keep them adequately and entertainingly supplied.

The disappearance of Martin Earnshaw did not fit any of these stereotypes. What made that case sexy was the victim's wife. Chloe Earnshaw was a waiflike blonde of steely determination on whom the media had seized from the moment her husband went missing. Her first press conference, at which, with glistening eyes, she hovered throughout on the edge of breakdown, made the national news on all channels, and from then on she never seemed to be off the screen or out of the papers.

What also made the public interest unusual was that no one knew for a fact Martin Earnshaw was dead. He had certainly disappeared under suspicious circumstances, he had certainly been under threat of death, but as yet no trace of his body had been found. Without the constant appearances of his photogenic wife asserting that he had been murdered, the public would soon have lost interest in the case.

Once Charles Paris had been cast in the role, he tracked down and read everything he could find concerning Martin Earnshaw's disappearance. This was not because he was under any illusions about the part. Dana Wilson had told him firmly that it didn't involve any speaking, so Stanislavskian efforts to get under the character's skin – even if Charles had been the kind of actor to indulge in such excesses – would have been pointless. No, it was just from interest that he delved into the Earnshaws' background.

What he found out was by then well known to any tabloid

reader. Charles Paris, always having been more of a *Times* man – and in fact a *Times* crossword rather than a *Times* news man – had been cheated of the more lurid details.

Martin Earnshaw was – or had been – in his fifties, a property developer based in Brighton. Hit hard by the recession, he had endeavoured to refloat his business by borrowing. Because the banks were unwilling to oblige, he had resorted to less respectable sources of funds and got into the clutches of a major-league loan shark.

As his repayments fell further and further behind, Martin Earnshaw had become the object of increasingly violent threats. A few weeks before his disappearance, he was found near his home with facial and abdominal bruising. A strong-willed man, he had apparently not buckled under in the face of these threats, but been determined to expose the extortioners. In fact, he made an appointment to tell a local detective inspector all the details.

That appointment was never kept. The night before it, a Wednesday in early October, Martin Earnshaw told his wife he was going out for a drink, and never returned. It was her assumption and everyone else's – probably even the police's, though they tended to play their cards closer to their chests than the tabloid press – that Martin Earnshaw had been murdered by the men he was about to shop.

All these details were related to the media by the doll-like figure of Chloe Earnshaw. She was his second wife, the first having died some seven years previously. It was a perfect marriage. Chloe was twenty years younger than Martin, they had been together for two years and – at this point during that first press conference the glistening, dark blue eyes began to spill – 'had been intending soon to start a family. Something which now,' she had continued, recovering herself with agonizing discipline, 'looks unlikely ever to happen.' She still hadn't lost hope of seeing Martin again, she insisted, but was prepared for the worst.

That worst, everyone knew – and indeed gleefully anticipated – was the discovery of her husband's body.

Official enquiries continued and grew in intensity. But as information dried up and leads proved abortive, the power of television was enlisted to help the investigation. The police, having tried themselves to reconstruct Martin Earnshaw's last evening without much success, had readily accepted *Public Enemies'* offer to reconstruct it for them.

This had necessitated a couple of days filming in Brighton, which was no hardship for Charles Paris. The town had always held a raffish attraction for him, full of memories of the one woman he'd made love to there, along with fantasies of all the other women he'd like to have made love to there. Was it a generational thing, he wondered, a post-war nostalgia, that still made Brighton's air, like that of Paris, heavy with sex? He had only to step out of the train from Victoria to feel the lust invade his mind.

The Black Feathers, in which Martin Earnshaw had last been seen, was in the hinterland of the Lanes between Royal Pavilion and seafront. It wasn't one of the highly tarted-up pubs of the area, but retained a proletarian – and indeed slightly deterrent – grubbiness.

The landlord and staff, however, had proved infinitely co-operative to the WET team, led by director Geoffrey Ramage. This was not pure altruism. While a positive disadvantage for someone trying to sell a house, murderous connections in a pub are good news for business. And if those connections are advertised to millions on nationwide television, the potential boost to trade is enormous. The viewing public is notorious for seeking out any location featured on the small screen, regardless of the context in which it was seen.

In the cause of verisimilitude, Geoffrey Ramage had asked the landlord to get together all the regulars who might have been present on the evening of Martin Earnshaw's disappearance.

To Charles's surprise, when he spoke to those who had been assembled, none had any recollection of seeing the missing man.

The actor's instinctive suspicion about this was quickly allayed by further conversation. It turned out that very few of the other drinkers had actually been there on the relevant night, but the lure of television coverage had prompted them to finesse the truth a little.

The sighting of Martin Earnshaw in the Black Feathers had not, as it transpired, come from one of the pub's regulars. An anonymous caller had passed on the information to Chloe Earnshaw, and this had been corroborated by a subsequent telephone call – also unidentified – to the police.

It became increasingly clear to Charles that the Black Feathers was in fact one of those pubs which doesn't have many regulars. In spite of the landlord's attempts to give the impression of a convivial community, the pub was – like Charles's own 'local' in Westbourne Grove – a joyless and anonymous environment.

The landlord himself stoutly maintained that he had seen the missing man sitting with two others on the night in question, though he was vague about further details.

Not for the first time, Charles had brought home to him the fallibility of human witnesses. Recollection is quickly clouded and distorted. From his own experience – and this wasn't just due to the Bell's whisky – Charles Paris knew how difficult he would find it to report accurately what he had been doing even a few days before. So the landlord's vagueness did not surprise him. Cynically, he even wondered whether the man was making up his story. From the point of view of trade, it was certainly in the interests of the Black Feathers that he remembered Martin Earnshaw.

Charles Paris's role in the filming was not onerous, though Geoffrey Ramage, in the self-regarding way of television directors, made as big a deal of it as he could. Dressed in clothes and fake Rolex watch identical to those worn by the missing man, Charles had to sit at a gloomy corner table with two other extras and drink. It could, uncharitably, have been called 'type-casting'.

There was an element of character-acting involved, though, because Charles had to drink draught Guinness rather than the more instinctive Bell's. This was on the advice of Chloe Earnshaw. Her husband, she insisted, had always drunk draught Guinness.

Having Chloe on hand did nothing to drive away the lustful thoughts which Brighton always inspired in Charles. She was there to advise on the filming and they had been introduced by Geoffrey Ramage in the lounge of the hotel that was the *Public Enemies* base.

In the flesh she was even smaller than her photographs and television appearances suggested, but somehow more robust, more curved, more tactile. She was simply dressed in black, as if already anticipating the news she feared to hear, and her blonde hair was scraped back into an artless ponytail.

A tremor ran through her when she was introduced to Charles and an involuntary hand half reached out to touch his arm. She gave a little shake of her head. 'I'm sorry. It's just . . . They've cast you very well. I mean, you don't really look like Martin, but there's something . . . Your height, the way you stand, it's . . .'

Tears once again welled up in the dark blue eyes. 'I'm sorry. I'm not being very brave.'

'Oh, but you are.' The words formed instinctively and were out before Charles was aware of them. 'I mean, you've been very brave from the start – coping with the trauma of your husband's disappearance. And then there's the risk you take by speaking out at all. The same risk that your husband exposed himself to . . . I mean, that is, assuming what you are afraid has happened to him *has* happened to him.' Her brow wrinkled in pain. 'I'm sorry, I'm saying all the wrong things.'

'No, no. Not at all, Charles,' she reassured him softly.

And Charles Paris was hooked. Just like the rest of the public. There was something mesmerizing about the woman's vulnerability. Anyone meeting her in ordinary circumstances would have found Chloe Earnshaw only moderately attractive. It was the knowledge of her jeopardy that gave her such charisma.

The onlooker was drawn to her, but at the same time felt guilty about being drawn to her. She looks fanciable, the thought process ran, but how awful of me to entertain ideas like that about a woman in such distress. It's dreadful to take pleasure from someone else's suffering.

Though of course the pleasure taken from someone else's suffering was the dynamo generating the success of programmes like *Public Enemies*.

Chapter Two

Charles Paris was used to the atmosphere of television hospitality suites, but this one was different. During the transmission of the first of the new series of *Public Enemies*, there was the usual undercurrent of showbiz excitement in the room, the usual panic elaborately disguised as cool, but there was also a more robust coarseness in the general badinage. It was because the police were there.

Public Enemies collaborated closely with the police – Bob Garston kept banging on about *how* closely they collaborated with the police – and the police took this as a licence to bring as many of their number as possible to the WET studios when the shows were being transmitted. Some of the force justified their presence – the on-screen presenters obviously, the police researchers, those uniformed figures bent over computers and telephones who filled out the background of the set – but others were just along for the ride, attracted by their colleagues' involvement, the glamour of television and the prospect of free drink.

Charles Paris was there just for the free drink. He'd been meant to be there working. Geoffrey Ramage, fresh from the excitements of the Brighton filming, had had Charles called for the live transmission. He was proposing a moody background silhouette of the actor dressed as Martin Earnshaw while Chloe did her latest heart-wrenching appeal.

Geoffrey Ramage was actually always proposing moody background silhouettes. Like all television directors, he really saw himself in the movies and, though his only actual experience in cinema had been doing soft porn, he had been bitten at an early age by the *film noir* bug. The opportunities to indulge this obsession in *Public Enemies* made him feel like a child with limitless credit in a sweet shop.

Charles's only brush with the genre had occurred when a seventies movie he was in had been hailed as 'a British homage to *film noir*' by a critic who didn't realize that the film's budget hadn't stretched to more lights. The actor's own contribution – a mere spit and a cough – had been characterized by the same critic as 'unthreateningly menacing', and Charles had spent a long time puzzling over whether that was a good notice or a bad one.

Geoffrey Ramage's moody background silhouette had been rejected by Bob Garston first thing in the morning, but since Charles Paris had been called, that meant he'd have to be paid another day's fee. The money was nothing to get excited about – Martin Earnshaw was unfortunately not called upon to speak in the reconstruction of his last known movements, so Charles Paris was being paid as a mere extra – but any money was welcome to his morbidly undernourished bank account.

Because he'd written off the day – and because there was the WET bar at lunchtime and the prospect of free hospitality later – Charles decided he'd stick around and watch the proceedings. Television studios are always full of so many people with unspecified roles that one more or less ligging around wouldn't provoke comment.

So he had a pleasantish day, watching the *Public Enemies* egos battle it out on the studio floor. Roger Parkes was the self-appointed voice of reason, Geoffrey Ramage the self-appointed *enfant terrible*, but Bob Garston rode roughshod over both of them. It was his show, and he wasn't going to let anyone forget it. With no attempt at tact or even awareness that other people might have opinions, the 'man of the people' continued on his workaholic course.

And Charles Paris sat benignly in the bunker of an audience

seat, watching the flak fly overhead. He liked the atmosphere of a television studio, and he liked it even better when he had no responsibility for anything that was going on in it.

The free hospitality, when it came, was a bit meagre. Commercial television companies used to lay on wall-to-wall food and drink, so that working on a production would ensure Charles didn't have to go near a supermarket for its duration. The ready availability of spirits even slightly diminished his Bell's whisky bill.

But the new austerity which followed the reallocation of their franchises brought ITV companies' generosity down to BBC standards – or even lower. The only foodstuffs on offer in the *Public Enemies* hospitality suite were crisps and nuts. The booze was limited to wine and beer. And, seeing how vigorously the police hangers-on were getting stuck into that, supplies weren't going to last very long.

Charles wondered whether this parsimony came from WET or from Bob's Your Uncle Productions. Given the way Bob Garston dominated all other aspects of the production, he probably also controlled the hospitality bill. Its niggardly provisions were certainly in character with his teetotal righteousness.

In the circumstances Charles Paris resorted to an old trick. He took a half-pint beer glass, filled it with wine and sat cradling it unobtrusively in the corner.

He needn't have worried about drawing attention to himself. The police contingent were far too caught up in their own banter and camaraderie to take any notice of anyone else.

There were about a dozen of them. Two were silent, though the remainder made noise enough for many more. Only a few were in uniform, but the others had that distinctive rectangular look which always gives away a policeman.

One of the silent ones was a thickset, mournful-looking man in his forties, who wore plain clothes and was tucking into the booze with a single-mindedness Charles could not but respect.

The other wore uniform, with a few extra flourishes on his jacket which presumably betokened higher rank, and sat apart from the rest, nursing a beer. He was an older man, probably round Charles's age, which in police terms must have put him near retirement. The attitude of his colleagues to him mixed a perfunctory deference with covert insolence. At times they seemed almost to be sending him up. From their banter Charles picked up that the man was called Superintendent Roscoe.

The mob reserved their greatest derision, however, for the colleagues who actually appeared on the screen, and here there was no attempt at concealment. The figure who provoked most raucous response was the one introduced by Bob Garston as 'our resident expert from Scotland Yard – Detective Inspector Sam Noakes'.

'Yeah, and we all know what she's expert in, don't we?' shouted one of the younger policemen.

'Will you let me take everything down for you and use it in evidence, Sam?' asked another fruitily.

'I'm afraid I must ask you to accompany me to the bedroom,' giggled a third, bowled over by his own wit.

The object of their offensive was certainly attractive, but there was about her a toughness which made Charles think they wouldn't have made the sexist remarks to her face. DI Sam Noakes had red hair and those pale blue eyes which the television camera intensifies. Though a detective, she wore uniform, presumably because she looked so good in it. The entertainment element is always paramount in programmes like *Public Enemies*, and there are a good few male viewers out there who are turned on by – and will therefore turn on for – a pretty woman in uniform.

Immediately she started speaking, it was clear that DI Sam Noakes was more than just a pretty face. She had a distinctive voice, deep, with a rasp of efficiency in it, as she enumerated the police successes prompted by the last series, and gave bulletins on the cases that remained unsolved. She was good, and her performance gained an extra glow from the fact that she knew she was good.

Even the sexist banter in the hospitality suite recognized her quality. Through the innuendo ran a thread of respect, at times verging on awe. DI Sam Noakes was already a power to be reckoned with inside the force before television brought her skills to a wider audience.

Public Enemies was scheduled at prime time, ITV Thursday evening, just after the nine o'clock watershed which in theory protected children from sex and violence – and in fact encouraged them to stay up and watch it.

The programme's format was a magazine. Live updates on cases, reports on stolen goods, reconstructions of crimes and appeals for witnesses were intermingled with more general features. These were mostly consumer advice, presented with that distinctive smugness which characterizes all television consumer programmes. The subjects covered might be a report on tests for home security devices, tips on how to recognize forged banknotes, lists of the right antique markets to check out for stolen property, and so on.

But for the first programme of the new series, *Public Enemies* did something different. As Bob Garston put it grittily (he put everything grittily – he was constitutionally incapable of speaking without grit): 'We've all watched a lot of television detectives, haven't we, and I'm sure we've all got our favourites. But in fictional crime there are two traditions – that of the professional police detective conducting an investigation and that of the gifted amateur doing the business. On the one hand we've got, if you like . . . Morse – and on the other, say, Poirot. Presumably, Sam,' he continued, turning a gritty smile on DI Noakes, 'Morse is a bit closer to the real world than Poirot?'

'Not that much closer, Bob,' she replied with a knowing grin. 'I still want to know how Morse gets hold of that car. Last time

I asked down the car pool for a red Jaguar, they laughed in my face.'

Bob Garston let out a gritty chuckle of complicity. 'Yes, but come on, Morse conducts his investigations with all the back-up of computer records and forensic laboratories. Surely that's a bit closer to real police methods than relying on "the little grey cells".'

'We don't actually call it "relying on the little grey cells", but if that expression means respecting intuition and responding to sudden lateral thoughts, then it's certainly a very important part of police investigation.'

'Good, thank you, Sam.' Bob Garston turned smoothly to another camera. 'Well, here on *Public Enemies*, we like to keep you up to date with everything about crime and its investigation, so we thought it'd be interesting to talk to an amateur sleuth, and maybe compare his methods with those of a professional police investigator. So I'm very glad to welcome to the studio – Ted Faraday.'

The shot opened out to include Sam Noakes and a rugged-looking man in his late forties, casually dressed in jeans and baseball jacket. 'Evening, Bob.'

This greeting prompted a roar of obscene responses from the hopitality suite.

'Now, Ted, would you say that your methods as an amateur—?'

'Sorry, I have to interrupt you there, Bob. That's twice you've referred to me as an "amateur". I'm not an amateur. I'm a professional private investigator.'

Bob Garston's face clouded. This was not how the item had been planned in pre-programme discussions, and it rather made nonsense of his neat link about Morse and Poirot. He shoe-horned a smile on to his face. 'All right, point taken. Would you say that your methods as a *professional private investigator* differ very much from those used by the real police force?'

Ted Faraday opened his mouth to reply, but before he could say anything, Sam Noakes interposed, 'I think it should be pointed out that Ted is an ex-copper, so his methods are based on the training he had in the Met, anyway.'

Bob Garston seemed glad of this support against Faraday. 'You two know each other?'

'And how!' shouted a raucous voice in the hospitality suite.

'Yes, we do,' Sam admitted.

Bob Garston turned his attention to the private investigator. 'Well, Ted, how do you react to what she says?'

'When I'm allowed to get a word in . . .' Ted Faraday began with lazy charm, 'I would like to say, yes, I was trained by the Met, and it did teach me some very useful lessons. I would also like to say that, now I'm outside the place, I realize just how rigid it is in its thinking, and how much easier it is to respond rapidly to situations without being strangled by bureaucracy when you're out in the real world.'

The discussion continued. Charles had no means of knowing their past history, but Sam Noakes seemed determined to score points off Ted Faraday. It made for a lively exchange, which climaxed when she coolly announced, 'I think this is all kind of sour grapes, Ted. You'd actually rather be back in the Met than faffing around on your own . . . assuming you still had the option.'

If ever there was a remark which demanded a follow-up question, that was it, but Bob Garston, concerned about the other items yet to be fitted into the programme, curbed his hard-bitten journalistic instincts and moved on to wrap up the interview.

In the hospitality suite, Charles learned a little more. Faraday was evidently well known to the police contingent and many of his exchanges with Sam Noakes had prompted jokes and barracking. After her last remark one of the policeman shouted, 'Well, you got to be a PI, haven't you, Ted? Should have realized the golden rule – if you want to stay in the Met, keep on the right side of the right people . . . isn't that right, Superintendent Roscoe . . . ?'

The superintendent looked up from his beer, whose level had gone down very little in the previous half-hour, and smiled. It was a complex smile. Within it were unease and caution, but also undeniably triumph.

'Hey, listen, listen!' shouted one of the policemen and attention returned to what Bob Garston was saying.

'. . . and we on *Public Enemies* are always trying to find out more about crime on behalf of you, the audience. So we thought we'd hire our own private eye and put him on the Martin Earnshaw case. Are you game to take up the challenge, Ted?'

'If you're prepared to pay my usual rates – plus expenses . . . you're on, Bob.' Faraday grinned. Clearly this part of the programme had been heavily set up.

Bob Garston turned to the detective inspector. 'And, on behalf of Scotland Yard, are you prepared to take up the challenge?'

Sam Noakes also grinned. 'Oh yes.'

'So we'll keep up progress reports here on *Public Enemies* and see whether the real police, with all the resources at their disposal, can be beaten to the solution by the gifted amateur!'

Ted Faraday again winced at the description and would probably have remonstrated, but Bob Garston had already turned to another camera and started reading his next link off the autocue.

The last item on that week's *Public Enemies* was another follow-up on the Martin Earnshaw disappearance. This, needless to say, featured the missing man's wife, currently Britain's favourite sufferer.

Geoffrey Ramage may have been denied the set-dressing of a moody Charles Paris silhouette in the background, but the effect he came up with was still pretty theatrical. Chloe Earnshaw, dressed again in simple black, was shot against a blown-up black-and-white photograph of the Black Feathers. The overhead lighting bleached the colour out of her hair and skin, so that only the deep blueness of her eyes disturbed the monochrome. The light also sparkled off her unshed tears.

What she said was the usual stuff. 'There must be someone out there who knows something about where Martin is. I appeal to them – I beg them – to tell me where he is or what's happened to him. Even if the news is bad, I want to know it. When I know, I can start to rebuild the rest of my life. Please, please, if anyone knows anything – the smallest, smallest thing about Martin . . . just pick up the phone.'

And all over the country men thought unworthily, 'I wouldn't mind picking up the phone and asking for her number.'

Charles had an unworthy thought too. There was no doubt that Chloe Earnshaw was one of those people whom, as the showbiz cliché has it, 'the camera loves'. Charles Paris couldn't help suspecting that the camera's devotion was reciprocated.

Chapter Three

DI Sam Noakes had changed into a figure-hugging red dress after the programme. Its colour had been carefully selected to complement rather than scream at her hair. Out of uniform, she still looked good, but softer, less of the disciplinarian.

Her appearance in the hospitality suite was greeted by a tide of catcalls and innuendo which washed off her unnoticed. The silent, heavy-drinking plain-clothes man turned towards her.

'Quite the television star now, aren't you?' he said. 'Police investigation meets game show, eh? What'll it be next, Sam – *Blind Date?*'

She looked at him coolly. 'Well, if it was, I'm afraid I wouldn't pick you, Greg.' It was spoken lightly, but the words stung. Before he could respond, she went on, 'Anyway, I'm a copper. All this television stuff is irrelevant – just means to an end. If it helps solve crime, then I'll do it.'

'Even if it means a "head-to-head play-off" against Ted Faraday?'

'Even if it means that.'

'And so you're doing all this in the line of duty? You don't get any buzz out of just being on the box?'

She shook her head decisively, setting the red hair swaying. 'I just get a kick out of doing my job well, Greg . . .' The pale blue eyes gave him an even stare. '. . . doing it as well as a man would.'

'Better than a lot of them.' The man called Greg looked across the room and murmured intimately, 'Oh-oh, talk of the devil.'

He moved out of the way as Superintendent Roscoe came across to Sam and embraced her with a clumsy, old-fashioned peck on the cheek. 'Another lovely performance, Noakes. Very well done indeed, my dear.' Charles saw her wince at the endearment, but the superintendent didn't notice. 'Whenever I watch this programme, I feel really glad that I backed the suggestion of doing it so strongly in the early days.'

'Yes.' DI Noakes sounded neither interested nor as if she believed him. Her eyes were already over his shoulder, searching out someone else to talk to. Superintendent Roscoe seemed to have the same effect on all his colleagues. Superior in rank he might be, but they all ignored him.

There was a commotion at the door, as more of the production team entered. Sam Noakes, taking advantage of the diversion with a murmured 'Excuse me', moved away from Superintendent Roscoe.

Charles Paris also moved. The booze was getting low and he wanted to ensure a refill before the new influx. He knew it was a bit unfair to take drink from the mouths of people who'd just been busting their guts in the studio, but there are extreme situations in which fairness cannot be the first priority.

He managed to drain what looked like the last bottle of red into his beer glass. That half-filled it, which would have to do.

He was moving away from the bar when he felt a tap on his shoulder. 'Ted.'

Charles turned to find himself facing the plain-clothes officer Sam Noakes had called 'Greg'. The man reacted with some surprise. 'Sorry, I thought you were Ted Faraday.'

'No, I'm Ted Faraday.' The real owner of the identity had just entered the suite.

'Yes, of course you are,' said Greg. 'Just from the back it looked ... Ted, this is, um ...' He didn't know the name '... the guy who played Martin Earnshaw in the reconstruction.'

'Oh, right.'

'Charles Paris,' Charles Paris supplied helpfully.

'Ah. Good to see you.' Charles felt his hand firmly grasped as the private investigator gave him a thorough look. 'Yes, not a bad likeness.'

'Just get you a drink, Ted.' Greg moved to the bar.

'Oh, thanks, I'll have a—'

'Be a matter of what there is, I'm afraid.'

Left alone with Faraday, Charles Paris felt the need to make conversation. 'You know anything special about the Earnshaw case?'

The investigator shrugged. 'No more than anyone else does. Till we find a body . . .'

'You think that's what will be found?'

'Oh yes, Charles. Somebody knows something. Scotland Yard wouldn't be taking a disappearance this seriously if they weren't pretty damned sure it's a murder.'

'And you think you'll find the body before the police do?'

'I'll give it a bloody good try. Probably easier for me to go underground than someone on the force.'

'But if you're reporting back on the programme every week, isn't it going to be difficult for you to go completely underground?'

'I'll file my reports by phone – or fax more likely. As with all these programmes, the skill is in how much information you give to the public.'

'Bob Garston gave the impression he wanted this story to run through the series. What happens if Martin Earnshaw's body's found straight away?'

A cynical smile tugged at the corners of Ted Faraday's lips. 'Be bloody inconvenient, wouldn't it? Murderers just have no sense of what goes to make a good television programme. Actually, though, there is a contingency plan for that.'

'Oh?'

'If they find the body, then the stakes go higher. It's a race between me and the Met to find the murderer.'

'Do you really approve of methods like this?'

The investigator screwed up his face wryly. 'Well . . . everything else is showbiz these days. Politics . . . the Monarchy . . . why should the police force be any different? And these programmes do sometimes turn up information you wouldn't get from any other source. Anyway, from my point of view, it's bloody marvellous.'

'Hm?'

'For someone who's only recently set up as a PI, this kind of publicity's like gold dust.'

'Yes, but publicity in your line of work could be a two-edged sword, couldn't it? Not much use having a face that's famous from television when you're doing undercover stuff, is it?'

'Don't worry about that. I am *a master of disguise.*' Ted Faraday rolled the cliché ironically round his mouth.

'And when your name's nationally known you'll get a whole lot more enquiries and bookings?'

'Reckon so. And another thing about *Public Enemies* employing me is—' Faraday grinned '—the money's bloody great. That is the big difference from the Met, let me tell you. As a PI, when you get the work, you get properly paid for it.'

'Very nice too.'

'You bet. No, I've really found my feet since I've been out of all that form-filling crap. I wouldn't go back into the real force if they asked me on bended knee.'

'No danger of that happening.' The new voice belonged to Superintendent Roscoe who had sidled into the periphery of their conversation.

Ted Faraday's reaction was interesting. He very positively ignored the superintendent and, talking into the empty air, announced, 'At least in the real world I don't have to deal with superannuated timeservers with no understanding of crime or criminal methods.'

The antagonism hung almost visibly between the two men. Superintendent Roscoe seemed for a moment to contemplate a riposte, but either he changed his mind or couldn't think of anything clever enough to say, because he lumbered off awkwardly to join the fringes of another group.

'Ex-boss?' asked Charles.

Ted Faraday grinned drily. 'You'd make a great detective, picking up subtle nuances like that. Actually, Shitface Roscoe is the reason I left the force.'

'Can I ask why?'

'Too complicated to go into. Let's just say a personality clash. You're never going to find much in common between someone with a bit of imagination and a talentless bureaucrat whose priorities are stifling initiative in others and taking any available credit for himself.'

'Ah,' said Charles Paris. Faraday's answer seemed to have covered the question pretty thoroughly.

The noise in the room abated as Chloe Earnshaw entered. Her television make-up was gone and she looked more vulnerable than ever, as though a layer of protective skin had been removed. There was a momentary hesitation among the policemen who towered around her, before the one Sam Noakes had addressed as 'Greg' moved forward protectively.

'Another very moving appeal, Mrs Earnshaw.'

She turned the blue eyes on him with an air of bewilderment. 'Just so long as it does some good.'

'Yes, of course. I think it's bound to.' He fell back on cliché. 'There must be someone out there who knows something.'

'I hope so.' She look gauchely round the room. 'I shouldn't really have come in here.'

Then why did you? Charles instinctively asked himself, surprised how readily Chloe Earnshaw had prompted another unworthy thought.

'I find crowds difficult at the moment,' she went on.

Then why do you walk into one? Charles's mind unworthily continued.

'Better than being on your own, though,' said Greg. 'At least you can't brood so much when you're with people.'

Chloe Earnshaw gave him a little wry smile, which seemed to announce her infinite capacity to brood in any circumstances.

'Come on,' he said gently, 'let's get you a bevvy.'

As he spoke, he took her arm and led her towards the drinks table. To Charles there seemed something oddly flamboyant about the gesture, as if it were made for the benefit of someone else. And from the glance Greg flashed towards her, that someone else appeared to be Sam Noakes. But either the detective inspector didn't see the move, or deliberately showed no reaction to it.

The noise level in the room rose again as Bob Garston entered, in the middle of an argument with Roger Parkes. Its subject was, needless to say, the programme and, also needless to say, Bob Garston was doing the talking.

'Listen, it's our job to keep *Public Enemies* one step ahead. We're not the only True Crime series on television at the moment, but we're the best and I'm bloody determined we're going to stay the best. We're not going to achieve that, though, if we fill the programmes with half-baked ideas and makeweight features.'

'The public are *interested* in automatic security lights,' Roger Parkes remonstrated wearily. 'It's just the kind of consumer information they want. And it's the kind of feature that's dead easy and cheap to set up and—'

'That's all you bloody think about, Roger – what's easy and cheap. And I'll tell you, items that're easy and cheap *look* easy and cheap. You may have swanned through your career at WET doing the minimum, taking the line of least resistance, but you're working with *Bob Garston* now. And I care about programmes that have my name on them. I work bloody hard to make myself the best I can be at what I do, and I demand the same kind of commitment from everyone who works for me – *everyone!*'

'But—'

'Even the bloody executive producer! I know that's a title that usually means bugger all – just a way of giving some talentless penpusher the illusion of usefulness – but when the production's one *I'm* involved in, then I see to it that *everyone* pulls their weight!'

'Bob, there's no need to be insulting. I—'

'Listen, television's a competitive business. We've got to do *better* than the opposition – doing *as well* as them is just not good enough. We've got to have new ideas, new approaches, new surprises. We've got to give the audience no alternative but to watch *Public Enemies*. They've got to watch the programme because they know they're missing something if they don't watch it. So we need a dynamic approach, not a line-of-least-bloody-resistance, let's-do-it-because-it's-cheap-and-easy approach!'

'I am giving you all the backing I can,' said Roger Parkes with some dignity, 'but we're only at the start of the series. We have to pace ourselves over the next six weeks. The production team have worked on overdrive for this programme and that's fair enough – it's the first, it needs to make an impact. But they can't maintain that level of energy all the time. We need a few – as you so sneeringly call them – *easy* items to lower the tempo a bit.'

'But we don't want to lower the bloody tempo – that's the way of mediocrity – and only a mediocre mind thinks like that!'

The executive producer was having difficulty curbing his anger, but he managed it. Charles could guess at the motivations which lay behind that restraint. Not least among them, he imagined, was the fact that WET needed *Public Enemies* for its ratings potential, and if that meant putting up with the manic bad manners of Bob Garston, then so be it. In the changed climate of television, when staff jobs hardly existed, when everyone was only as good as their last short-term contract, the replacement of an executive producer was easily achieved. If he was going to keep his job, Roger Parkes could not risk upsetting the applecart.

'Very well,' he said in a conciliatory tone which must have cost him a great deal. 'I'll see to it that everyone gives you all the back-up you require, Bob.'

'Good.' Garston was momentarily appeased, until he saw Geoffrey Ramage entering the hospitality suite and went straight back on to the attack. 'And that everyone includes the bloody director!'

Ramage looked bewildered, still dazed from the exhaustions of the studio day. 'What?'

'*Public Enemies*,' the presenter fulminated on, 'is a piece of serious factual reportage. Its basis is no-nonsense hard-bitten journalism – it's not an excuse for some bloody wanker to audition for the Fritz Lang School of Hardboiled Realism!'

Before Geoffrey Ramage had time to respond to this assault, Bob Garston was interrupted by one of the lumbering policemen. 'Hey, the booze has run out. Who's the person who sorts that kind of thing out round here?'

Roger Parkes replied instinctively. He might have a mediocre mind, he might never have made the greatest creative contribution to television, but he was highly skilled in the most important part of a producer's role – getting drinks for people. 'I could organize some more supplies from the bar,' he said.

'No,' said Bob Garston.

'What?'

'Bob's Your Uncle Productions are controlling the budget on this show. We've allocated a certain amount for hospitality. If that's finished, then that's finished.'

'What, you mean you're not authorizing any more booze?' asked Roger Parkes in disbelief.

'Exactly,' Bob Garston replied with gritty relish.

It must be wonderful, Charles Paris thought wistfully, genuinely not to care whether people like you or not.

The WET bar was closed by the time the full impact of the hospitality suite drought had sunk in, so it was a somewhat disconsolate group of policemen and production staff who trickled out of WET House at the end of the studio day. Some left for public transport, some went to their own cars, others had hire cars organized. There was an official-looking vehicle with uniformed driver for Superintendent Roscoe. And something very close to a limousine waiting for Bob Garston. Whatever budgetary restrictions might apply to other members of the production team, he was a man with star status to maintain.

Charles Paris found himself shuffling through the main door in a group which included Sam Noakes and Ted Faraday. Outside he encountered a phenomenon he hadn't expected for what was basically a documentary series – autograph hunters. The overlap between police work and showbiz was becoming total.

The current focus of their attention was Chloe Earnshaw. She was being fittingly modest, saying 'Oh, you don't want my autograph', but clearly they did. She looked interrogatively at one of her police minders, who shrugged and said, 'Don't want to antagonize them.' So, with a show of reluctance, Chloe Earnshaw signed the few books and bus tickets that were proffered, before being whisked away by her minders to 'a secret location'. (The threats that had been made to her husband and the public way in which she attacked their perpetrators ensured that she was under twenty-four-hour police protection.)

The autograph hunters turned next to the emerging group and there was no doubt who they were after in that lot. However much she dismissed the possibility, in the public imagination

DI Sam Noakes had become a star. Hers was the name they wanted in their collections.

One of them asked Ted Faraday for an autograph. He refused, firmly but without rudeness. 'Sorry, in my business you sign as few things as possible.'

'Afraid someone might track you down through your handwriting?' Sam Noakes asked teasingly.

'Maybe.'

'Or – even more worrying – find out your real character through it?'

'Always a risk,' he responded with a lazy grin. There was definitely some undercurrent beneath their banter, though its precise nature Charles could not define.

'Did they organize a car for you, Ted?' Sam asked.

'Offered one. I told them not to bother. Never like being committed to where I'm going to be at the end of an evening.'

Some transient message flashed between their eyes. 'They've done a car for me,' she said casually. 'Fancy a lift?'

Matching her casualness, the private investigator accepted the offer. Charles was aware of a sound behind him and turned to see Superintendent Roscoe and Greg who had just come out of WET House. They had both heard the last exchange and neither looked particularly pleased about it.

'Good night, Superintendent. Good night, Greg,' Sam called over her shoulder, as she moved elegantly towards the hire car.

Superintendent Roscoe waved an acknowledgement, but the other policeman said nothing. Nor did Ted Faraday, as he nonchalantly followed the female star of *Public Enemies* into her car.

The autograph hunters lingered, hoping to catch Bob Garston when he came out. They'd have a long wait. The presenter had dragged Roger Parkes and Geoffrey Ramage straight down to an editing suite, to watch and make notes on a playback of that evening's *Public Enemies*.

The autograph hunters didn't ask for autographs from Superintendent Roscoe or the man called Greg.

Nor, it goes without saying, from Charles Paris.

Chapter Four

Got to be masochism, hasn't it, thought Charles as he dialled Maurice Skellern's number. I mean, why else would anyone go on ringing someone whose news was always depressing? He tried to think of a single occasion when an unsolicited call to his agent had left him feeling better, but his memory drew a blank. There had been instances – rare instances – when he had rung back after a message from Maurice and received good news, but a call out of the blue had never prompted more than gloomy reflections on the current 'quietness' of the business and on Charles's failure to 'make anything happen for himself' in his chosen career.

He was therefore surprised when he got through to hear his agent in a state of considerable excitement.

'You've no idea, Charles,' Maurice bubbled on, 'how gratifying it is for someone in my profession when all your efforts finally pay off.'

'What?'

'When a talent which you have been nurturing for years – nurturing – finally gets the recognition it so richly deserves. I mean, it makes it all worthwhile – all the anguish, all the hours you spend on the phone trying to make producers aware of your client's skills, all the afternoons when the phone doesn't ring once, all the occasions when you despair that the client's ever going to take any initiative ... well, let me tell you – when there's a really big breakthrough, you forget all that.'

'And has there been a really big breakthrough?' asked Charles, trying to sound cool, almost uninterested.

'Oh, I would say so. Yes, I most certainly would say so. No two ways about that.'

'How big?'

'Only *internationally* big. Only *globally* big. Only – and I breathe the word with appropriate respect – only *Hollywood* big.'

'Really?' Charles murmured, hardly daring to believe his ears.

'Columbia Pictures . . .' Maurice Skellern continued in a deliberately matter-of-fact tone, 'Columbia Pictures, no less, are doing a remake of *The Spy Who Came in from the Cold* – you remember the movie?'

'Of course. Richard Burton.'

'Exactly, Charles. Exactly. Richard Burton as the fiftyish, over-the-hill, crumpled, down-at-heel, unsuccessful spy. Only one small problem – Richard Burton's dead.'

'Yes. I did hear that.'

'So Columbia wants the new Richard Burton. But not a Richard Burton who's already an established star. They want to *create* the new Richard Burton – find the right person and rocket him to stardom. So their casting people get working and they start looking for someone who can play fiftyish, over-the-hill, crumpled, down-at-heel, unsuccessful. And – inevitably, because of the way he puts himself about in the business – they end up ringing Maurice Skellern. Hello, they say, have you got anyone on your books who can play fiftyish, over-the-hill, crumpled, down-at-heel, unsuccessful? Well, yes, I reply, as it happens I do have on my books the perfect person to play, fiftyish over-the-hill, crumpled, down-at-heel, unsuccessful. And the rest, as they say, will be history.'

Charles could hardly find enough breath in his lungs to murmur, 'So what's the next step?'

'I've shown the Columbia people over here the photograph – they're happy. I've sent them the showreels of work by the actor in question – they're happy. The next step will be to fly him over to Hollywood for final interviews.'

'When?' asked Charles, thinking of the infinite void that was his engagements diary.

'Tomorrow.'

'Oh, my God. It's wonderful news, Maurice, isn't it? I mean, sensational news. Best news I've ever heard in my life.'

'That's very sweet of you to say so, Charles. I'll pass it on to Malcolm. He'll appreciate it.'

'Malcolm?'

'Malcolm Tonbridge. You remember. You met him once at my office.'

'Malcolm Tonbridge? But he's hardly forty, is he?'

'Thirty-eight.'

'And he's not crumpled. I mean, he's quite good-looking.'

'Very good-looking. Positively dishy. That'll stand him in good stead in Hollywood, you know.'

'Yes, but I mean, the part surely demands—'

'Hollywood knows what it wants, Charles. Good heavens, you can't have a character who's meant to be fiftyish, over-the-hill, crumpled, down-at-heel, unsuccessful played by someone who actually *is* fiftyish, over-the-hill, crumpled, down-at-heel, unsuccessful, can you?' Maurice Skellern let out a wheezing laugh. 'Otherwise, well . . . otherwise even *you'd* be in with a chance, eh, Charles?'

The wheezing laugh continued. Maurice was tickled pink by his little fantasy. It was the best joke he'd thought of for a very long time.

Indulge the masochistic mood while it lasts, thought Charles, as he dialled the number of his wife Frances. 'Ex-wife' would perhaps be more accurate. Though there was still no official divorce, the 'ex'-ness seemed to be hardening increasingly into permanence.

'Hello?'

'It's me. Charles.'

'Oh yes?' Long experience of such phone calls had brought her response to the point where it had no intonation of any kind. 'What can I do for you?'

'Just rang for a chat.'

'Ah.' There was a silence. 'A chat about anything in particular?'

'No. Just . . . you know . . .'

'I don't know unless you tell me, Charles.'

'No. Well, I . . . Just to see how you are and . . .'

'Fine. I'm fine.'

'Good.'

'You?'

'Oh, fine, yes. Yes, fine, thank you.'

'Any work?'

'I have actually just done a job.'

'Well, there's a novelty.'

'One of those *Public Enemies* programmes.'

'When's it going to be on?'

'It was on. Last night.'

'Oh. Well, sorry. I missed it.'

'There you go.'

'Charles, if you don't tell me things're coming up, how am I expected to know—?'

'Sure, sure. Sorry, I should have told you, but . . . the filming kept me very busy,' he lied.

'Hm. What were you doing in the show?'

'I was in one of the reconstructions,' he admitted shamefacedly.

'Charles . . . After all the things you've said about people who get involved in that kind of stuff . . . Last time the subject came up, I seem to remember you talking about "actors whose only previous work has been in dandruff commercials".'

'Yes, well, you know . . . No one'd ever offered me a reconstruction before.'

42

'Hm. So now I just have to wait and I'll see you in a dandruff commercial, is that it?'

'No one's ever offered me one of those either,' he said, with an attempt at humour.

'But if they did, you would instantly say yes – as you do to everything else.'

'Oh, I don't know. I'd like to think . . . Yes, I probably would,' he conceded lamely.

'Really, Charles. Why you can't get a hold on your career and . . .'

She gave up. What was the point of going through all the old arguments again? Raking over old embers. It seemed a long time since those embers had contained even the smallest spark.

Charles could sense her thoughts. Or perhaps he was just transferring his own on to her. Either way, they made him feel achingly empty.

'What were you playing in the reconstruction?' she asked.

'Murder victim. Well, to be accurate, *probable* murder victim. Martin Earnshaw.'

'Oh.' Frances sounded touched. 'Husband of that poor girl who . . . ?'

Charles was surprised that Frances too was under the spell of Chloe Earnshaw. He could understand the male population of the country, but he'd always had great respect for his wife's bullshit-detecting antennae. Probably he was just being over-cynical again. God, why couldn't he take anything at face value? Why couldn't he trust or believe in anything?

'How's work for you?' he asked, trying to shift his developing mood.

'Do you really want to know?'

'Well . . .'

'It's OK. The school is still standing. I'm still its headmistress. I could provide more detail, but I know you're not really interested.'

43

'Well, now, I wouldn't say . . .'

It was another sentence not worth finishing. Frances was right. He wasn't really interested in the minutiae of staff-room politics.

'So . . . ?' She made the word sound like a sigh.

'So,' he echoed. He had had thoughts of fixing a time to meet, asking her out somewhere, but the sterility of the conversation sapped his will. What *was* the point? They really had grown apart now. Separate people. With separate lives. Linked only by a few ambivalent memories. Even those were fading.

And a daughter, of course. Yes, they were linked by a daughter. He was on the verge of asking about her, but again what was the point? He knew Frances would only remind him that he had Juliet's phone number and was quite capable of ringing her himself. The emptiness ballooned inside him.

'Well, anyway, Frances . . . As I say, I just rang to see that you're OK.'

'And, as I say, I'm fine.'

'Yes. Well . . . I'll be in touch.'

'Fine.'

'Goodbye then, Frances.'

'Goodbye, Charles.'

Was he being hypersensitive, or had she put the phone down more abruptly than was strictly necessary?

Charles mooched disconsolately along the landing towards the door of his bedsitter. There was the remains of a half-bottle of Bell's in there. At least he thought there was. On those days when he started sipping early, it was always difficult to remember how much there was left.

He was stopped by the sound of the phone ringing. To his amazement, it was Maurice.

The agent's mood had changed totally, its previous euphoria supplanted by a dull gloom.

'What's the matter?' asked Charles.

'Malcolm Tonbridge. Bloody Malcolm Tonbridge.'

'What about him?' A churlishly appealing thought insinuated itself into Charles's mind. 'Columbia haven't gone off the idea, have they?'

'Oh no, Hollywood are as keen as ever. Keener if anything.'

'So?'

'Malcolm just rang me. Said now his career's taking off, he needs to be with a bigger agency.'

'Oh.'

'People who specialize in movies. People who've got "representation on the West Coast". He said he was grateful to me for all I'd done for him, but he's moving into a very specialized area and he needs to be looked after by specialists.'

'I see.'

'God, Charles, I feel a complete failure.'

'Well, I'm sorry, Maurice. But why on earth did you ring to tell *me* about it?'

'Because, of everyone I know, you're the one person who I thought'd really *understand*.'

'Oh,' said Charles Paris, 'thank you *very* much.'

Chapter Five

Once, in a moment of eloquence assisted by Arthur Bell's distillery, Charles Paris had defined the life of an actor as like that of a child's glove puppet, spending most of its life crumpled and forgotten in the corner of a toy cupboard, and only fully alive when a warm hand was inserted into it. At the time the references to inserting warm hands into things had triggered a burst of crude innuendo, but Charles still thought there was something in the image. The hand of course, which animated the actor's personality, was work. Give an actor a job, and suddenly he exists.

Pursuing this image through, it could be said that Charles Paris spent the four days after the first *Public Enemies* programme crumpled up and forgotten in the corner of a toy cupboard. He had made the necessary – or perhaps unnecessary – phone calls, to Maurice and Frances, on the morning after, and didn't feel inclined to ring either of them again. From his agent he would only get more unwittingly dismissive references to his own career and reproachful catalogues of the perfidies of Malcolm Tonbridge.

And from his wife he would get . . . He didn't quite know what he would get, but he didn't relish it. Something basic seemed to have changed in his relationship with Frances. Ever since he'd walked out – and indeed for much of the twelve years before – the marriage had been an on–off affair, but in the past he had always felt confident that any 'off' would eventually give way to an 'on'. That core of certainty had now gone. The relationship had descended to a new bleakness, and the cold prospect that they might permanently lose contact had become increasingly feasible. Maybe Frances, finally and irrevocably, had had enough of him. Ringing her again would only increase the pain.

He could have telephoned other friends, suppressed his envy to those who had work, indulged in mutual moaning with those who hadn't. He could even have arranged to meet some of the unsuccessful ones, and continued the moaning over too many drinks somewhere. But it all seemed a lot of effort.

So it was the crumpled glove puppet in the corner of the toy cupboard. He was not completely inert. He made it to the overpriced corner shop to buy the basic necessities for his solitary menu, in which toast, baked beans and breakfast slices figured more prominently than most *chefs de cuisine* would recommend. He also stocked up on the necessary bottles of Bell's.

Once or twice, driven by some childhood Calvinist conviction that drinking on one's own was a bad thing, he adjourned to the pub. But the one he always went to, in Westbourne Grove, was, like the Black Feathers, 'local' only in geography. The bar staff, Australians who had always started the job that day, had a religious objection to recognizing anyone over thirty.

And the older customers, some of whose faces Charles had seen before, evidently came to the pub for a mystic private communion with their drinks. After twenty minutes sitting shrink-wrapped in his own isolation amidst the music and shouts of the young, drinking alone appeared an infinitely more sociable option.

How long this torpor might have continued was impossible to know, because it was interrupted on the Tuesday morning by a dictatorial phone call from Louise Denning. Charles was commanded to attend a briefing meeting at WET House that afternoon. As usual in the medium, it was assumed that no one would have any more pressing calls on their time than the demands of a television programme. Charles, who of course *had* no more pressing calls on his time than the demands of a

47

television programme, would nonetheless have preferred the summons be couched as a question rather than an order.

'Well, I am free as it happens,' he conceded after some invisibly mimed diary-consulting, 'but I thought I'd finished my bit.'

'There has been a new development in the case,' Louise Denning announced mysteriously.

'Am I allowed to know what it is?'

'No. You'll be given all necessary information at the briefing meeting.'

'Oh. Does this mean that I'm going to be involved in more filming? That I'm being booked for this week's show too?'

But Louise Denning was too canny to answer the actor's instinctive question. Though the old-fashioned BBC tenet that an offer of work made over the phone was tantamount to a contract had, in harder-nosed commercial times, gone the way of most 'gentlemen's agreements', incautious words could still pose a risk. 'I'm afraid I'm unable to answer that, Mr Paris,' the researcher replied primly. 'But I'm sure everything will be made clear at the meeting this afternoon.'

They're so bloody arrogant, thought Charles, as he put the phone down. They think everyone'll just drop everything to turn up to their bloody meetings. No contract, no talk of payment, and they expect me just to appear on the off chance. I've half a mind not to go.

But, needless to say, the other half of his mind won. He appeared meekly at WET House in very good time for the three o'clock meeting.

There's something very pervasive about policemen. They quickly colour the ambiance of any situation in which they are involved, and the briefing meeting at WET House that afternoon was a case in point. The television people – almost all the *Public Enemies* production team – easily outnumbered Superintendent Roscoe, DI Noakes and the man called 'Greg' (who was now

48

identified as Detective Sergeant Marchmont), but the way the three of them sat behind a long table immediately transformed the atmosphere into that of an official police briefing. Even Bob Garston's ego was subservient to the professionals.

Not that the first professional to speak was particularly charismatic. Superintendent Roscoe liked the sound of his own voice, but nobody else appeared that keen on it. The production crew shifted without interest in their seats, and his two colleagues avoided each other's eyes, afraid their superior's long-winded oratory might set them giggling.

'And,' the superintendent announced, homing in on his subject after some five minutes' preamble, 'we – that is I – have taken an unusual decision in these changed circumstances. I have decided that the news should be embargoed until Thursday's transmission of *Public Enemies*. This is not done simply to give the programme an exclusive publicity coup . . .'

Though, from the gleeful expression on the face of Roger Parkes, it would certainly do that.

'. . . It is because I have decided that, in my judgement, a shock announcement of that kind will be the most effective way of advancing our enquiries. The relationship between the police and the media has not always been as smooth as one might wish, but here is an occasion where we can mend a few fences by a bit of mutual backscratching. *Public Enemies* will benefit from the exclusive we are offering, and we in the police can hopefully also benefit from the new information that will come in as a result of these disclosures. I have decided that this is the best way for us to proceed, and I will stand by my decision in the face of any opposition.'

You didn't have to be a very sophisticated psychologist, Charles reckoned, to conclude that someone who asserted so often a decision had been his own was clearly talking about a decision made by someone else.

Bob Garston had been silent too long. *Public Enemies* was his

49

show, after all, and he couldn't allow anyone else more than a brief appearance centre stage. 'Of course, Superintendent, the main opposition we're likely to encounter will be from the boys in News.'

'Of course. This is the kind of information that would normally be broken in a news bulletin, but I have decided it will be more effectively used in your programme. I have no doubt it's the kind of decision that will cause a bit of a furore.'

'That's an understatement,' said Roger Parkes jubilantly. 'ITN will be extremely shirty about this – so will the BBC. It'll get all kinds of flak from the press and could even lead to questions in the House. But don't worry, I'm prepared to defend my decision.'

Oh, I see, so it's *your* decision now, thought Charles. Since the previous Thursday Roger Parkes had changed, seeming to have grown in stature. He even appeared less deferential to Bob Garston, as if he had gained a new ascendancy over the presenter. Charles wondered if it was Parkes who had actually broached the idea of the news embargo and *Public Enemies* exclusive to Superintendent Roscoe. That would explain his new chirpiness – and also create something of a precedent in television – an executive producer coming up with a good idea.

Roger Parkes immediately confirmed Charles's conjecture, as he continued, 'I knew what the stakes were when I first put forward the suggestion, Superintendent.'

Roscoe coloured. He didn't like having the initiative taken away from him in this way. DI Noakes even more studiedly avoided DS Marchmont's eye. The showing-up of their superintendent was clearly regular enough to have become a running joke between them.

'Still, we'd better move on,' said Roscoe brusquely. 'Noakes, over to you.'

She was ready, as ever poised and efficient. Immediately, the audience listened. Superintendent Roscoe didn't carry authority; Sam Noakes did. 'Right, so you've all got the background. What we're dealing with here is extremely secret information. Our approach – embargoing it until it's announced on *Public Enemies* on Thursday – is risky, and it's only going to work if we can guarantee absolute security from everyone involved in the production. You're only here because you're all people who will have to know what's happened in order to do your jobs making the programme.

'But, if that programme's going to happen as we want it to, you're all virtually going to have to sign an Official Secrets Act. If a murmur of this gets to the press before Thursday, a lot of people are going to be left with a lot of egg on their faces. So I want you all to be aware just how high the stakes are. Don't breathe a word of it to anyone – however close they are to you, however much you trust them. If this scheme's going to work, secrecy has to be total – do you all understand that?'

There were murmurs of assent from around the room. Television people love a good internal drama; and the more that drama relies on restricted information, the more they love it. This one promised to be even more exciting than gossip about who'd lose their job next.

'Well, OK,' said Geoffrey Ramage, 'you can rely on all our discretion, no problem about that. We won't tell a soul about the new information, but' – and here he voiced the question of everyone in the room – 'can you please tell us what that new information is?'

'Yes,' said Sam Noakes, professionally slowing the pace of her revelation. 'Of course. We have had a significant breakthrough in our investigations into the disappearance of Martin Earnshaw. Last night in a—'

'Excuse me,' said Sergeant Marchmont. 'Sorry to interrupt, Sam, but we agreed to operate this thing on a "need to know" basis.'

'So?' She was put out at having her narrative interrupted.

'So . . . there are people in this room who already know all they need to know.'

'What? Who?'

The detective sergeant consulted a list on a clipboard. 'The actor Charles Paris.' Charles looked up in amazement as Marchmont continued, 'He's going to be involved in further filming reconstructing Martin Earnshaw's movements and it's important he understands how secret that is. You do understand that, do you, Mr Paris?'

Greg Marchmont looked round the room to locate the actor.

'Yes, yes, I understand that,' Charles assured him.

'No mention to anyone of where you're doing the filming, no mention even that you're doing it at all – OK?'

'OK. Won't breathe a word to a soul.'

'Someone on the production team'll let you know where you've got to be tomorrow.'

'That's right,' Louise Denning agreed, brusquely efficient. 'You'll get a call at home later on this afternoon.'

'Fine.'

'But that's all you need to know, Mr Paris,' said Sam Noakes, happy to regain the initiative from Sergeant Marchmont.

'You mean I don't get to find out what this new information is?' asked Charles plaintively.

'Sorry. You'll have to wait till nine o'clock on Thursday – along with the rest of the population.'

'Oh. Oh.' Charles rose to his feet. 'So now . . . I just go, do I?'

Sam Noakes flashed him a professional smile. 'Please.'

Sidling out of the conference room, Charles Paris felt like the boy not picked for either side in playground football. As he opened the door, the unworthy thought of listening at the keyhole crossed his mind, but the presence of a uniformed officer in the corridor put paid to that. The security on this edition of *Public Enemies* was being taken very seriously indeed.

Charles felt extraordinarily frustrated. It was like getting to the end of a thirties detective story and finding the last few pages torn out.

Still, he thought philosophically, there are compensations. First, I will be working again tomorrow. And, second, I have been expressly forbidden to tell anyone I'm working. So maybe I can get away without paying any commission to Maurice Skellern.

The high level of security was maintained during the following day's filming in Brighton. The substantial police presence which kept the general public away from Charles Paris showed just how seriously they were taking it. Nothing would be allowed to leak before the transmission of *Public Enemies* the following evening.

Charles's actual filming was scheduled for after dark, but he was booked for the full day. This he didn't mind at all, as it meant overtime. At ten a car picked him up from Hereford Road to drive down to Brighton. He had assumed that it was one of the hire cars regularly used by WET, and was surprised to discover the driver was a policeman. Presumably this was another reflection of the high security surrounding the operation.

Once in Brighton, Charles was smuggled into the same hotel as before and put up – though he couldn't keep the phrase 'holed up' out of his mind – in a private suite. Here he met Geoffrey Ramage and other members of the *Public Enemies* team, as well as even more policemen. Charles got quite a buzz out of the situation, all the cloak-and-dagger secrecy reminding him of a post-*Ipcress File* espionage movie in which he'd had a small part. It had secured him a memorable notice from the *Observer*: 'Charles Paris's character looked so confused by all the crossing and double-crossing that the bullet which put paid to him on the Berlin Wall must have come as a merciful release.'

53

A lavish room-service buffet was laid on, but Charles regretfully rationed himself on the free wine. He was, after all, working. The surrounding policemen showed no such inhibitions. It seemed that the line Charles had said in so many stage thrillers, 'No, thank you, sir, not while I'm on duty', was yet another fabrication of crime fiction.

After lunch the reason for his early call became apparent. It was not that his portrayal of Martin Earnshaw required greater psychological depth than it had the previous week, simply that on this occasion the character had to walk. Being filmed sitting in a pub drinking called for limited skills of impersonation, whereas movement needed coaching. To this end, Geoffrey Ramage insisted that Charles watch videos of the missing man.

The only available footage dated from Martin Earnshaw's first marriage, inept wobbly shots of him acting up for the camera on holiday in Majorca. The property developer was then presumably benefiting from the boom of the early eighties. He looked very happy and carefree, anyway, with an almost childlike innocence about his clowning.

Charles wondered idly what had happened to the first marriage. If he had been investigating Martin Earnshaw's disappearance, that was certainly something he would have looked into. But it was a safe assumption that the combined intellects of the entire police force and Ted Faraday had already made that mental leap and acted on it. Charles, who had in his time been involved in investigating a few crimes, was rather enjoying his current position on the periphery of one but without personal involvement.

Martin Earnshaw seemed to walk like most other people of his age and build, but Charles patiently – and literally – went through his paces for Geoffrey Ramage, making minuscule adjustments to stride length and arm swing as required. After an hour or so, the director was satisfied.

To Charles it all seemed a bit pointless. Given Geoffrey's

tastes in lighting, he knew that on the final print 'Martin Earn-shaw' would appear as little more than a blur.

The evening's task, when it was spelled out to him, did not promise to stretch Charles Paris as an artiste. He had to leave the Black Feathers, and walk – in the approved Martin Earnshaw manner – through a few dark alleys and lanes to the seafront. Once there, he had to walk down on to the beach underneath the Palace Pier.

That was it. Hardly King Lear, but, from an actor's point of view, the part did have a couple of things going for it. First, there were the free meals. And, second, no other actors were involved. It was a one-man show.

Charles was interested to find out the source of the new information about his *doppelgänger*'s movements. So great had been the appeal to the British public of Chloe Earnshaw's television appearances that her own home telephone had been constantly ringing with offers of new leads. Since many of the potential informants had rung off when answered by a policeman, it had been decided to return Chloe from the 'secret address' to her home. Here she was left on her own, though under heavy surveillance, to answer the telephone. All calls were recorded by the police and checked for authenticity.

The details of Martin Earnshaw's route from the pub to the Palace Pier had come from a woman who refused to give her name. In fact Chloe Earnshaw had been out shopping when the call came through and it was recorded on the answering machine.

The voice quality was muffled, as if the caller had been resorting to the old B-feature cliché of a handkerchief over the receiver. The woman had given no clues to her identity, and police thought it probable that she shouldn't have been in Brighton at the relevant time. Possibly she'd been with a lover. Perhaps she even had some connection with the people responsible for Martin Earnshaw's disappearance. Certainly her muffled message gave the police no means of tracking her down.

Her information, though, they took very seriously, which was why Charles Paris was made to retrace the route she outlined. After the filmed insert had been played in on the following night's *Public Enemies*, Bob Garston would do another of his impassioned, straight-to-camera pleas.

'We do need the woman who gave that information to come forward. We will ensure absolute secrecy for her, but there are a few more follow-up questions we need to ask. Please. We know you're out there somewhere. You've already done the public-spirited thing once by giving that information. Please don't be afraid. Call us again. Who knows, you might be able to tell us that one little, apparently insignificant, detail that enables us to catch these . . . "Public Enemies"!'

For Charles Paris the filming was frustrating. Not because of the actual work – anyone capable of copying Martin Earnshaw's walk could have done that – but because of the knowledge that all the crew around him knew the details of the revelation to be made on the following evening's programme.

He tried, with varying degrees of subtlety, to elicit the odd hint from Geoffrey Ramage, from the cameraman, the Make-Up girl, the police who kept the public away from the location. Not one of them cracked. They'd all taken Sam Noakes's words to heart. The security screen was impenetrable.

Charles Paris, even though he *was* Martin Earnshaw, would, in common with the rest of the British population, have to wait till nine o'clock on Thursday to find out what had happened to the missing man.

Chapter Six

He was not called for the following day, so there was no way that Charles could once again see *Public Enemies* in the comfort of a WET hospitality suite. In common with nine million other members of the British public – or more if Roger Parkes's optimistic prognostication proved correct – he would have to watch in the comfort of his own home.

'Comfort' was not a word readily applied to Charles's Hereford Road bedsitter. He had moved in there when he left Frances, and the room still appeared to be in mourning for their marriage. Maybe Charles had once entertained fantasies of a slick interior-designed bachelor pad to which an endless succession of glamorous women could be lured, but if so, reality had quickly quashed such ideas.

He'd never been good at home-making, drifting before his marriage from one anonymous set of digs to another, rarely bothering even to unpack. Frances it was who had brought into his life the concept of a home as more than somewhere to sleep. She had also introduced him to a love of possessions – not for their monetary value but as a cement of memories, mutual purchases marking off the phases and moods of their marriage.

With the marriage, however, all that had ended. The shared mementoes stayed in their Muswell Hill marital home, an unfinished collection frozen reproachfully in time. And when Frances had finally moved out to her flat in Highgate, many of them just disappeared. Reproducing the same acquisitiveness in his own environment, or even making that environment a little less squalid, would have felt to Charles like a further betrayal of his relationship with Frances. Some perverse, self-punishing instinct dictated that as he had made his bed, so must he lie on it. Except that he very rarely did make his bed when he wasn't changing the sheets. And he didn't do that as often as he should have done.

The room therefore had never fulfilled its promise as a seducer's silken lair. Though Charles had not been without female company since the end of his marriage, not many of the encounters had been conducted on his home ground. Few women had actually been inside the bedsitter. Which was probably just as well.

So it remained very much as it had been when he moved in, all those features about which he'd thought 'that's the first thing I'll change' still unchanged. The grey-painted furniture, the yellow candlewick bedspread bleached now to an unhealthy cream, the sad curtain hiding sink and gas ring, the customary accumulation of glasses and brown-ringed coffee cups – everything gave off a miasma of defeat. It was an appropriate setting for Charles Paris in empty-glove-puppet mode.

That was the state in which he spent the Thursday, trying to pretend he wasn't infected by the same prurient interest as the other nine million who were waiting to watch *Public Enemies*.

His television was of a piece with the rest of the bedsitter – an old portable dating from the days before beige plastic had been appropriated exclusively for computer monitors. To its top was attached a ring aerial, which needed constant realignment to minimize the snowstorms that flurried across the screen.

By the time nine o'clock arrived, Charles found he had got through nearly half a bottle of Bell's, which was bad, even by his standards. Still, it's justified, he thought. I deserve a bit of a celebration. I am, after all, about to watch myself on television. But even he wasn't convinced by such sophistry.

As the applause for the preceding sofa-bound sitcom gave way to a teaser for *Public Enemies* and commercials, Charles realized that once again he'd omitted to tell Frances he was about to be on television. But he didn't feel inclined to do so now. Instead, he poured himself another substantial Bell's.

The credits for *Public Enemies* combined urgency and threat. Crime scenes of mounting violence were superimposed on each other against insistent background music in which jangling guitars mixed with electronic sirens and gunshots. In each of the scenes the criminal appeared as a black void, an evil outline punching, stabbing or slashing at a blurred victim. These outlines froze in place until they all conjoined and blacked out the screen. Over this the blood-red *Public Enemies* logo suddenly appeared.

The blackness melted to blue and fragmented into new outlines, this time of anonymous policemen and women. Out of the middle of this montage a new image took shape and, just as the blood-red words 'with BOB GARSTON' appeared at the bottom of the screen, revealed itself to be a stylized picture of the presenter at his most no-nonsense, hard-bitten and journalistic. It was the gritty face of a man working at the coalface of real life.

The message of the credits was undoubtedly the one that Bob's Your Uncle Productions intended – only one man can find a solution to the rising tide of violent crime in this country, and that man is Bob Garston.

Charles Paris took a long cynical swallow of Bell's, as the image dissolved to zoom in on the real Bob Garston, live in the WET studio. He sat perched grittily on a high stool, wearing glasses for extra *gravitas*. His light double-breasted suit was beautifully tailored, in a way that eschewed dandyism and maintained the necessary grittiness quotient. It was certainly – and literally – a cut above the square-shouldered suits of the plainclothes men who were part of the presenter's backdrop.

Behind Bob Garston the WET designer had created a simulacrum of a police incident room, full of telephones, computers, maps and wall charts. Throughout the programme this area was criss-crossed by policemen and women, some in uniform, some not, but all possessed by a desperate urgency to fulfil some unknown mission. The constant, purposeless movement would have been extremely irritating if the viewer saw too much of it, but that was not a problem in a Bob Garston production. Characteristically, the presenter saw to it that he was held in tight close-up for all of his links.

Garston began the programme with even more concerned dramatic urgency than usual. 'Good evening. Tonight on *Public Enemies* we bring you exclusive news on a case that has had the country holding its breath for the past few weeks – the disappearance of Martin Earnshaw. In what is a first for a non-News television programme, *Public Enemies* will bring you information which Scotland Yard have kept secret from all other media until now. We will also get a reaction from Martin Earnshaw's wife to the new breakthrough. That's in a moment, but first a follow-up on last week's report about the security van robbery in Ilford . . .'

The hook had been baited, the promised revelation cunningly designed to keep millions of hands from straying to their remote controls for the next half-hour. No doubt Roger Parkes hoped that all over the country, extra viewers were being called in from the kitchen. 'Hey, *Public Enemies*'s got something new on the Martin Earnshaw case – and they're going to have that dishy wife of his on again. Bet they've found the body. Come on, love, come and see what's happening.'

The intervening items in the programme seemed particularly dull that week. Bob Garston had even allowed in Roger Parkes's survey of automatic security lights. But the relative tedium was calculated. Between each insert, the presenter wound up the expectation a little more, professionally controlling his revelations with all the skill of a strip-tease artiste.

At last the moment came. Turning with hitherto unplumbed

depths of grittiness to another camera, Bob Garston announced, 'And now we come to the latest news on the disappearance of Martin Earnshaw.' But he didn't go straight to the bombshell; still he extended his titillation of the viewing millions. 'We've had a great many very useful calls from members of the public offering new information – and don't forget, our phone lines are open now and continue to be open twenty-four hours a day. The number's on your screen, so if you know anything – anything at all – get in touch. Remember, even what seems to you an insignificant detail could be vitally important to the police investigations – so please pick up your phone.

'We've had one very useful call from a lady who saw Martin Earnshaw leaving the Brighton pub where the previous last sighting of him occurred. She's given us invaluable information for which we're very grateful, but we would urge her to make contact again to . . .' And he went into his predictable routine before introducing the reconstruction.

Charles Paris watched his own performance dispassionately. The only emotion it aroused in him was mild distaste. Was it really for this that I became an actor? The world is full of wonderful parts in brilliant plays and I end up imitating the walk of a vanished property developer. Have I no pride? Is there no job I wouldn't do for money?

Uncomfortably suspecting that he knew the answers to the last two questions, Charles Paris refilled his whisky glass, which seemed unaccountably to have emptied itself.

At the end of the insert, Bob Garston still prolonged the agony. There were repeated pleas for anyone with information to come forward, further specific pleas to the woman who had seen Martin Earnshaw going to the Palace Pier. Then there was a reminder about the challenge between Ted Faraday and the police from the previous week's programme, and the news that the private investigator had faxed in an update on his progress.

'He's gone undercover, but is very optimistic that he's getting somewhere with his investigations.'

Bob Garston paused and held the silence for a long time. Then, turning to yet another camera, he produced his *coup de théâtre*.

'However, Ted Faraday is probably not yet aware of the dramatic new development in the case. I am able to tell you – here, exclusively, live on *Public Enemies* – that a body has been found, which is believed to be that of Martin Earnshaw. Or to be more accurate, *parts* of a body have been found.'

He left another long pause for the gruesome impact of his words to sink in even to the slowest viewing intellect. 'Over to Detective Inspector Sam Noakes for the details.'

The camera found her at the front of the busy incident-room set. She sat, sternly pretty in her uniform, at a functional desk. The camera homed in to exclude the meaningless bustle behind her.

'Acting on an underworld tip-off,' Sam Noakes, with effortless mastery of the autocue, announced, 'police went to a graveyard in the village of Colmer five miles north of Brighton, where there had been apparent desecration of two recent graves. This kind of crime is all too common at the moment, and is frequently thought to be related to black magic practices . . .'

My God, this story's got everything, thought Charles. All we need now is a coven of naked witches. But his attempt at wry detachment didn't work. He was as surely ensnared by Sam Noakes's narrative as the rest of the silent millions.

'It was found on examination that two recently buried coffins had been tampered with. When opened, police did not discover any harm or desecration to the bodies inside. However . . .' The detective inspector may have claimed the showbusiness element of her work was merely a means to an end, but she could still hold a pause like a theatrical dame. '. . . they did discover that something else had been placed inside the coffins.' Another silence Edith Evans would have killed for. 'In each coffin they found a human arm.'

Millions of pins, in sitting rooms around the country, could have been heard to drop. Bob Garston gave them time to descend, before he again picked up the narrative.

'Preliminary tests on those severed limbs suggest strongly that they belonged to Martin Earnshaw. His wife has very bravely been to try to identify them and is also of the view that they belonged to her husband. Chloe Earnshaw is obviously deeply traumatized by the experience, but has still agreed to appear – here, live – on tonight's programme. Her reason is a belief in human justice. Her husband has been murdered, and Chloe Earnshaw is determined to help find the "Public Enemies" responsible for the crime!'

The grieving wife – now officially the grieving widow – appeared on a separate set, looking frailer than ever between two huge villainous black cut-outs like those in the credits. She was still an elegant figure, in black polo-neck sweater and trousers, the colour now justified by her new status.

Her thin face, again with pale hair scoured back, bore witness to the strain she was under. It seemed even thinner and the highly developed skills of television make-up could not hide – or had perhaps been under instructions from the production team not to hide – the deep circles beneath Chloe's eyes and the redness that surrounded them.

This evidence of her distress made even more unworthy Charles Paris's thought that she still looked fanciable. His guilt was only alleviated by the knowledge that the same unworthy thought had sprung up in a few million other male minds across the country.

'My husband has been murdered,' Chloe Earnshaw began simply. 'That is a terrible truth for any wife to come to terms with, and I don't think it's yet sunk in for me. The reason I feel strong enough to be here tonight talking about Martin is probably that the truth hasn't sunk in yet.

'But the reason that I am here talking to you is that I'm angry. Somebody has taken away the life of the man I love. They've taken him away from me forever. I'll never see Martin again.'

Her voice wavered as the reality of this hit her for the first time. She gulped and recovered herself. 'But I don't believe anyone should be allowed to get away with a crime like that. There still is justice in this country and I want the people who killed my husband to face that justice. They must have friends. They must have wives, girlfriends. There must be someone out there who knows who they are. Please, please, if you know anything . . . just . . . get . . . in . . . touch . . .'

The last words struggled out against a mounting tide of tears and, as they finished, Chloe Earnshaw slumped, her head in her hands, weeping bitterly.

The camera, which had closed in on her suffering face, drew back very slowly, till her tiny body dwindled and the two huge cut-outs of 'Public Enemies' seemed to fill the screen.

Then there was a surprise. Across that stricken image, with no signature tune, the credits started to roll. This was unprecedented. Never before had a production involving Bob Garston ended without a return to the presenter for a closing remark and reminder whose show it was. But in this instance, recognizing the strength of the final image, he must have put dramatic television above personal aggrandizement.

It was a surprising decision, given its source, but the right one. As the end credit, 'A WET PRODUCTION IN ASSOCIATION WITH BOB'S YOUR UNCLE PRODUCTIONS FOR ITV', rolled off the top of the screen and Chloe Earnshaw's tiny white face was lost in black, no one could deny the power of the image.

Nor could anyone deny the power of Chloe Earnshaw's performance. The actor in Charles had to admit, with purely professional admiration, 'She's bloody good.'

Chapter Seven

Roger Parkes's hopeful prognostications were gratifyingly realized. *Public Enemies'* revelations achieved all the reaction he had hoped for. The Friday's tabloids wallowed in the gruesomeness of the Colmer graveyard find, as ever appealing to that instinct in their readers which forms queues near motorway pile-ups, and as ever dressing up this prurience with 'the-public-must-be-told-the-truth' sanctimoniousness.

There even developed a race between the papers to find a perfect nickname for the crime's perpetrator. The *Mirror* led off with 'The Deadly Dissector'; *Today* offered 'The Sick Surgeon'; while the *Sun* kept things characteristically simple with 'The Bloody Butcher'. Having made their pitches, they sat back and waited to see which name the public would latch on to, each paper hoping that its coining might attain the mythic status of a 'Black Panther', a 'Moors Murderer' or a 'Yorkshire Ripper'.

The sensational Sunday papers, given more time, were able to come up with elaborate features on the story. The *People* brought forward a stomach-turning serialization of a forensic pathologist's memoirs; while the *News of the World* included a pull-out supplement on other murders involving dismemberment – which no doubt led to many tasteless jokes over Sunday joints.

Far more gratifying, however, to the *Public Enemies* team than this news-inspired coverage was the media reaction to the way the revelation had been made. As Roger Parkes had hoped, there was an explosion of affront from the 'quality' press and television news departments.

ITN attempted through the courts to put an injunction on

Public Enemies, prohibiting any further 'exclusive revelations'. *The Times*, in a leader headed 'THE TAIL WAGGING THE DOG', waxed lyrical about 'the sanctity of objective factual reporting' which must be protected from 'the iconoclastic vandalism of thrill-seeking entertainment programmes'.

To complete Roger Parkes's happiness, a question was actually asked in the House. A self-important Labour member from South Wales asked whether 'the Government condones the usurpation of journalistic values by televisual sensationalism'. Unfortunately the question received no meaningful answer, since it was asked at one of those moments when the chamber was virtually empty, but nonetheless a point of principle had been established.

Best of all, from the point of view of WET and Bob's Your Uncle Productions, that Thursday's edition of *Public Enemies* got wonderful 'overnights'. These were the first indications of audience share, ratings which would be confirmed by fuller research a week later, but which indicated that all the elaborately teasing trails running up to the programme had done their stuff. 'The BBC News,' as Bob Garston announced with relish, 'was bloody nowhere – hardly on the map. We bloody stuffed them!'

And, given the amount of publicity that week's programme had generated, the next week's *Public Enemies* looked set fair to stuff the BBC even more comprehensively.

Which was, after all, the whole aim of the exercise.

Charles Paris found it odd being dead. Previously his rendering of Martin Earnshaw had been an impersonation of someone who might or might not have suffered a dreadful fate; now suddenly he was playing a murder VICTIM.

It wasn't of course the first time he'd done that. He'd been killed off early in many creaky stage thrillers, notably one called *The Message is Murder* at the Regent Theatre, Rugland Spa. For another, whose title he had mercifully forgotten, he received a notice which claimed: 'Charles Paris dead was infinitely more convincing than the rest of the cast alive.'

Nor had his defunct performances been confined only to potboilers; he'd also given of himself in the classics. Indeed, his Ghost in a Chichester production of *Hamlet* had been greeted by the *West Sussex Gazette* with the following: 'Charles Paris, as the Prince's father, looked surprisingly corporeal. His too, too solid flesh certainly showed no signs of melting.'

But all these experiences were different from playing the part of a real person who had, until very recently, been breathing, walking and talking. And had now suffered dismemberment. Being Martin Earnshaw did give Charles a bit of a *frisson*.

But it's an ill wind ... Martin Earnshaw's murder offered Charles Paris the prospect of continuing employment – at least until the perpetrator of the crime was uncovered. The *Public Enemies* production team had come up with a winning formula, in which the heart-rending Chloe Earnshaw and her late husband were essential ingredients. They weren't about to change that in a hurry. Charles Paris, as the dead man, had become a running character in this soap opera of murder.

Briefly he even contemplated getting on to Maurice Skellern and demanding more money now he was such an integral part of the show, but he decided against it. Instead he – and some bottles of Bell's – passed the weekend around Hereford Road in empty-glove-puppet mode, waiting for the next summons to WET House.

It came on the Monday morning. Louise Denning, earnestly humourless, announced that he was required for a briefing meeting at eleven the following day. There was no enquiry as to whether he was available. It was again assumed that nothing would impede the ultimate imperative of television.

WET Reception was expecting him and Charles Paris was speedily and efficiently escorted upstairs by one of the programme secretaries. Once in the *Public Enemies* outer office, he was asked to wait. He was offered a cup of coffee, though no explanation for the delay. He accepted the coffee, which the secretary quickly brought before disappearing on some unspecified errand to another part of the building.

Charles was left alone, wishing he'd thought to bring his *Times*, so that he could have a crack at the crossword. But he hadn't. He looked around the office for other reading matter. There weren't even any programme files. The conspiratorial secrecy which surrounded *Public Enemies* ensured that all its records were kept under lock and key in an inner office.

Nope, he could see nothing that contained words except for the telephone directories and, compulsive reader though he was, Charles Paris wasn't about to start reading them.

He tried to find something else of interest in the room, but without success. Characterless grey walls and white ceiling; grey desk and typing chair; two low grey armchairs, on one of which he sat; grey telephones, photocopier and fax machine. It was the kind of decor that would have confirmed Kafka's worst fears.

Just as he was thinking that time and life were frozen, that nothing in the world would ever move again, he was surprised by a click. A slight whirring followed, as the fax machine burst into action.

For maybe a minute Charles convinced himself that he would be virtuous and not give in to curiosity. But he was alone in the office, and he was human. He moved casually across to the fax machine and squinted down at the emerging sheet.

The originating fax number began '0273', which Charles had dialled often enough to identify as Brighton, and the ident read 'PRINTSERVE'. Presumably some public fax bureau.

The typed message was short.

'GOING UNDERCOVER IN BRIGHTON. FOLLOWING UP VERY PROMISING NEW LEADS. TELL SAM I'M WAY AHEAD OF HER. REPORT AGAIN SOON. T.F.'

Charles didn't think it would be leaping to conclusions to assume that the fax came from Ted Faraday. So, even though the missing persons case had now developed into a murder hunt, the *Public Enemies* contest between the amateur and professional detectives was still on.

A door opened and Charles moved guiltily away from the fax, fascinated suddenly by some detail on the wall calendar. 'Come through,' commanded Louise Denning, never for a second contemplating any apology for keeping him waiting.

The customary level of television manners was maintained inside the room. Bob Garston and Roger Parkes did not even look up when Charles entered, but continued their latest squabble about programme content.

'Well, I still think,' the executive producer was insisting, 'that child abuse is exactly the kind of subject *Public Enemies* should be tackling.'

'Oh yes,' the presenter countered. 'If it's the right sort of child abuse.'

'What do you mean – the right sort? Surely child abuse is child abuse?'

'No, I mean, if we're going to have child abuse on a programme I'm involved in, then it's got to be sexy.'

'But, Bob, for heaven's sake – child abuse is sexy by definition.'

'No, it isn't. It's sex*ual* by definition. I'm talking sex*y*. *Public Enemies* doesn't want to show yet another kid, shot in silhouette or with the face electronically scrambled, moaning on about how her stepfather touched her up. The public's sick to death of it – they can get all that at home.'

'But child abuse is a criminal offence, and it's a major contemporary social problem.'

'Leave major contemporary social problems to BBC2 and Channel Four – we're talking mainstream television here.

Through this Martin Earnshaw thing we've got *Public Enemies* into a ratings position other factual programmes would kill for, and I'm not going to have that threatened by your mimsy-pimsy *Guardian*-reading conscience.'

'It is not just my conscience, Bob, it's—'

'Anyway, there are other programmes that have cornered the market in child abuse. God, I don't want to go into the ring with Esther Rantzen. I do have some standards.'

That final assertion was arguable, Charles Paris reflected, as Roger Parkes picked up the argument again. 'You take my word for it – research shows that child abuse is something the viewers are really concerned about.'

'I don't want them bloody concerned! I want them fascinated, I want them frightened, I want them hooked! While I'm on the screen, I want them to keep watching, I want them to keep their hands off the bloody remote control, for Christ's sake!'

'But—'

'And they're not going to keep watching yet another hushed-voice account of some kid's suffering at the hands of the family pervert. I tell you, nowadays child-abuse victims are as much of a turn-off as . . . fly-blown babies starving in Africa. Nothing's going to get the viewing public excited about child abuse victims . . .' Bob Garston paused as a new thought came into his mind. '. . . unless of course we reconstructed some of the actual acts of abuse . . .

'But no, we couldn't do that,' he concluded regretfully. 'Might look as if we were being exploitative.'

'But couldn't we—?'

Bob Garston signalled the end of the conversation by looking up at Charles. If he ever had known the actor's name, he'd certainly forgotten it. 'Right, you're going to be needed for more filming this week.'

Charles managed to bite back the instinctive reaction, 'Oh,

70

good.' Instead, he asked, 'Why, have you got new information through from the public?'

Bob Garston wrinkled his nose without enthusiasm. 'Not that much. Plenty of calls, of course, but all pretty bloody vague. No detailed stuff or positive sightings.'

'So there isn't much else you can do with me, is there . . . ?'

'Don't you believe it. We're on to a winner here. We're getting some pretty positive research from your appearances on the show.'

'Oh, thank you,' said Charles, flattered – as any actor would be – by a commendation of his performance.

Bob Garston's next words, however, took some of the shine off the compliment. 'No, apparently the viewers get quite a charge from having a reconstruction of someone who's actually been dismembered.'

'Oh,' said Charles Paris.

A wistful longing came into Bob Garston's eyes. 'Wouldn't it be great if another bit of the body gets discovered in time for this week's programme . . .'

'Mm,' Charles agreed with a chuckle. 'Maybe the murderer will have the good sense to feed the remaining joints out gradually over the next four weeks – so that you'd have one for each programme . . .'

'Yes . . .' The presenter of *Public Enemies* was far too absorbed by this delicious fantasy to realize it had been proposed as a joke. A dreamlike quality came into his voice. 'Yes, wouldn't that be just perfect . . .'

Roger Parkes decided it was time to assert himself. 'So, about this week's filming, Mr Paris . . .'

Bob Garston, fearful of any challenge to his command, snapped out of his reverie. 'Yes, about this week's filming. Though we've done Martin Earnshaw in the pub, and we've done him leaving the pub, we still haven't done him leaving home and getting to the pub.'

'Ah. Right. So that's what I'll be doing, is it?'

'Yes. Good thing is we can get Chloe in this one too.'

'Oh?'

'Well, the research on her is still very positive. Getting stronger every week.' Garston looked thoughtful. 'She really has got something, you know . . . I'd like Bob's Your Uncle to set up another project with her when this lot's finished . . .'

Charles was incredulous. 'Her own series, you mean?'

'Mm.'

'But wouldn't that require her having a different husband murdered every week?'

Bob Garston looked up sharply, touchy about the possibility of being sent up. 'Look, you just do your work as a bloody extra! Keep your wisecracks to yourself!'

'No, I didn't mean—'

'Another thing . . .' Roger Parkes chipped in, maintaining the admonitory tone of the conversation. 'The security on this show is getting more and more important. You mustn't breathe a word to a soul about what you're up to.'

'I haven't. I wouldn't.'

'Not even to a wife, girlfriend. No pillow talk – OK?'

'It's all right. I live alone.'

'Oh, that's a blessing.'

Depends on your point of view, thought Charles wistfully.

Bob Garston once again hijacked the conversation from his executive producer. 'Right, so we're pretty sure we're going to get very positive viewer reaction from having you in a reconstruction with Chloe.'

'But aren't you in danger of blurring the distinction between fantasy and reality?'

'Exactly.' Garston nodded vigorously. 'That's one of the main aims of programmes like *Public Enemies*.'

Chapter Eight

An unmarked police car arrived at Hereford Road the following morning to take Charles back to Brighton. It was larger than the previous one, almost a limousine. While I was just a missing person, he thought wryly, I didn't qualify for this. Now I'm officially a murder victim, nothing's too good for me.

But he was quickly disillusioned of the idea that the special treatment was just for him. In the back of the car, separated from the driver by a glass panel, sat Superintendent Roscoe and Greg Marchmont. The detective sergeant looked ill at ease, subdued perhaps in the presence of his superior, but Roscoe was almost excessively affable.

He wasn't in uniform, but quickly explained his pale trousers and diamond-patterned pullover. 'Mixing business and pleasure for a couple of days. Keep an eye on the television lot and maybe fit in a bit of golf. Got my clubs in the back, you know. Get ready for retirement, eh? Just think about it, Marchmont, in a few months I'll be able to do this every day . . . while you lot are still grinding away at the coalface.'

He chuckled. This was a new Superintendent Roscoe, different from the touchy and ignored figure seen before. Charles got the feeling it was Greg Marchmont's presence that had made the change. With Ted Faraday or Sam Noakes and most of the other police, the superintendent had seemed awkward, aware of their contempt. Detective Sergeant Marchmont apparently didn't have that power. In their relationship, Roscoe called the shots.

Certainly the junior officer remained awkwardly silent for

most of the journey, only speaking when politeness left him no alternative.

Superintendent Roscoe, on the other hand, was in expansive mood. 'I think this case is going to be my last triumph before I go, you know,' he announced.

Marchmont said nothing, so Charles filled in the silence. 'The Earnshaw case, you mean?'

'Yes. I've a feeling we're very close to the perpetrator.'

'Really? And is that thanks to the television programmes?'

'Well, they don't do any harm, but when this case is finally solved, it'll be down to good old traditional police methods.'

Marchmont stirred a little uneasily at this. Roscoe responded immediately to the unspoken criticism. 'No, I'm fully aware of all the new technology and that – very clever stuff. Genetic fingerprinting, offender profiling, new techniques in forensic pathology, computers, computers and more computers – all very helpful in their proper place. But they're no substitute for the instincts of an experienced copper.'

From the way he said it, Superintendent Roscoe clearly put himself into this category. 'Young sparks like Noakes and her mates,' he continued, 'are very talented. In a few years they'll be excellent coppers, no question, but right now I'd back someone like me against them every time. They'll start to make real progress when they twig that science can only do so much. There's got to be an intuitive mind working with all that science.'

'But Sam Noakes said as much,' Charles objected. 'On the first programme, when Bob Garston was talking about "the little grey cells", she said the police had to respect intuition.'

'She may have said it, but she doesn't put it into practice. At times when I've passed on my hunches to her, she's been downright rude about them.'

Greg Marchmont again shifted his considerable bulk. Charles surmised that it was the nature of Superintendent Roscoe's 'hunches' rather than the principle of respecting intuition that

Sam Noakes didn't like. He also got the feeling that, if she'd been there, Roscoe's defence of his old-fashioned methods wouldn't have got such an easy ride.

'You can have too much science,' the superintendent went on. 'When something's obvious, you don't need to go on wasting valuable resources to produce scientific proof that it's obvious.' Again Marchmont's body language suggested that, in different circumstances, he would have contested this assertion.

Roscoe continued, relishing the docility of his audience. 'I mean, take the arms that were found at Colmer . . . OK, you do the basic checks – blood group, that kind of thing – but the most important identification is always going to come from Chloe Earnshaw recognizing that they belonged to her husband. Once you've got that, then that's all you need to know.'

Charles thought it was perhaps time to stem the flow of generalizations. 'But surely there's other information that forensic tests can establish? Not just the identity of the victim, but the manner of his death, clues to where it may have taken place, how the body was dismembered, all that kind of stuff . . . ?'

Superintendent Roscoe shrugged. 'Oh yes, fibres from a carpet made in Taiwan and only fitted into a limited edition of thirty-four 1978 Cortinas – that what you mean?'

'Well, there have been famous examples of criminals getting caught on just that sort of evidence.'

'And there have been a darned sight more *less* famous examples of criminals getting caught because an experienced copper has used a bit of gumption.'

'How would you define "gumption"?'

'Common sense. You look at the available information – the broad outlines, not the molecular structure of every speck of dust found on the corpse – and you start to get a feeling of the kind of mind you're up against.'

'The murderer?'

'Right.'

75

'But surely that's what profiling does. I mean, criminal psychologists work out—'

'You don't need a criminal psychologist to do it. That's the point I'm making, Mr Parrish—'

'Paris, actually.'

'What?'

'My name's "Paris".'

'Oh, right. Well, Mr Paris, I'm saying that anyone of reasonable intelligence who's spent his working life dealing with murderers can produce you a profile at least as well as a bloody criminal psychologist can – except that the copper'll do it a lot cheaper and a darned sight quicker.'

'So have you worked out a profile of Martin Earnshaw's murderer?'

'Course I have.' The superintendent grinned smugly. 'The man who did it—'

'You're sure it's a man?'

'Oh yes. He's very clever – highly intelligent character we're up against here. Also he's a bit of an exhibitionist. He didn't dismember the corpse for the purposes of concealment. Oh no, he did it so that he can control the pace of the investigation. He's going to feed out bits of the body when he feels like it.'

Bob Garston's dream come true, thought Charles, and that prompted him to say, 'So presumably the murderer's delighted by the coverage he's getting on *Public Enemies*?'

'You bet he is, Mr Paris. He's enjoying all that very much indeed. You see, as I say, he's highly intelligent and he likes pitting himself against other intellects. He was always going to be doing that with the police, but now he's also challenging the combined intelligence of the entire television viewing public.'

Charles was tempted to say 'Not much contest', but bit the words back. 'Traditionally, exhibitionists like that tend to get caught because they become over-confident, don't they, Superintendent?'

'Yes, I would agree. Part of the thrill for that kind of murderer is seeing how close to the wind he can sail. He loves almost boasting about his crime, almost actually telling people he's done it and, as you say, it's that temptation that often leads to his downfall.'

'So do you reckon that's what'll happen in this case?'

'Maybe.' The superintendent tapped his teeth reflectively. 'I've just a feeling this murderer may be a bit too canny for that.'

'So do you think you'll get him?'

Superintendent Roscoe beamed a complacent smile on Charles. 'Mr Paris, I told you – this case is going to be the triumph of my career.'

Greg Marchmont again moved uneasily. He wasn't the only member of the force, Charles concluded, who would be relieved when retirement finally came for Superintendent Roscoe and his dated attitudes.

In Brighton the car drew up outside the same hotel they had used the week before. Probably WET had some mutually back-scratching discount scheme with the place.

The two policemen and the actor got their luggage out of the boot and carried it inside. Superintendent Roscoe's golf bag was a huge leather job with a zipped hood. It looked brand-new and was evidently its owner's pride and joy. Roscoe refused the hotel porter's offers of assistance, insisting on carrying it himself.

Inside the hotel foyer, Greg Marchmont looked round without enthusiasm. 'Back a-bloody-gain.'

'It's been a week,' said Charles.

'For you it may have been. I was here yesterday. Up to town last night, down here again this morning – like a bloody yo-yo.'

'You were following up on something yesterday, were you?'

The clam-up was instantaneous. 'Sorry, I can't tell you.'

'Sorry, I shouldn't have asked.'

The detective sergeant gave him a bleak smile. Charles noticed how tired and tense Marchmont looked. The case – or perhaps some other pressure – was taking its toll on him.

They went to Reception to check in. Whether being dead had actually enhanced his status or not Charles didn't know, but that week he got a much better room, complete with sea view and minibar.

Geoffrey Ramage and the WET camera crew were already there. After lunch (in which Charles, relaxing into his role, indulged himself a little more than the previous week) there was some more walking practice to recapture the definitive Martin Earnshaw gait. The director was not easily satisfied and kept making him do it again, but Charles knew this was simply to kill time. Martin Earnshaw had left his home for the last time at seven in the evening, so the WET crew couldn't start shooting until it got dark. Fortunately, in the intervening four weeks the evenings had drawn in and they left the hotel round four.

The Earnshaws' house was on the borders of Hove, all very middle class and discreet. So middle class and discreet that the setting up of cameras and lights elicited not the slightest reaction from the neighbours. This was in marked contrast to what would have happened in most residential locations. Anything to do with television usually draws an instant crowd.

Still, nobody was complaining. This middle-class restraint of curiosity made Geoffrey Ramage's job a lot easier, and rendered redundant Greg Marchmont and the other policemen delegated to guard the location.

When they arrived at the house, Charles was interested to notice the detective sergeant give a tiny nod of acknowledgement to an apparently empty van opposite. No doubt inside it some of his colleagues were maintaining twenty-four-hour surveillance on Martin Earnshaw's widow.

Chloe, as ever in equal parts fragile and tactile, was expecting them and let them into the house. She neither welcomed the intrusion nor resented it, apparently resigned to the necessity of turning yet another knife in the wound left by the murder. Again she greeted Charles, identically dressed to her husband when last seen, with a piercing, anguished stare. And again his response was unworthy.

Geoffrey Ramage took them quickly through the required actions, with Chloe occasionally interrupting to correct some detail of what was to be reconstructed. Charles found this a new, and rather unnerving, experience. To have Martin Earnshaw's actions described to him by the director was one thing, but to be taken through them by the dead man's wife was something else entirely. Charles was made very sensible of that element in *Public Enemies*, the blurring between fantasy and reality, which Bob Garston so prized.

They were only going to reconstruct what could have been seen from the street. Charles found himself wistfully – and it must be said, again unworthily – dwelling on what Chloe and her husband might have got up to inside the house in the moments before his departure. Why was it this woman always brought his thoughts back to sex? He didn't exactly fancy her, and yet he could not ignore her strong erotic aura.

Still, even the bit seen from outside involved her giving him a goodbye kiss and, as they rehearsed this, Charles realized gleefully that he would be fulfilling a national fantasy. When the reconstruction appeared on Thursday's *Public Enemies*, men all over the country would be envious of Charles Paris.

The kiss, though Chloe insisted on proper lip contact and even a hug and a little pat on the bottom from him, was strangely asexual. It wasn't just because of the circumstances, the lights, the camera crew. Charles had rehearsed enough stage kisses not to be expecting any major excitements. But he was still surprised at how cold and positively antaphrodisiac Chloe Earnshaw's lips proved to be.

Oh dear, he berated himself, another unworthy thought. The

woman had just been widowed in appalling circumstances. What was he expecting – that she'd suddenly demonstrate seething passion to a total stranger? He felt guilty and chastened by his reaction.

Charles Paris's latest performance as Martin Earnshaw did not involve much. He had to open the front door, succumb to the kiss from Chloe, and walk off down the road, turning once to wave as she closed the door.

This action, it was hoped, would be the latest prompt to the collective television-viewing memory. Had anyone out there witnessed the scene? Had anyone who had witnessed it seen some other significant detail . . . like, say, a couple of heavies with butcher's knives lurking in the shadows? Given the apparently total lack of interest in the affairs of others manifested by the Earnshaws' neighbours, it looked unlikely that anyone would come forward.

Still, audience research had shown flashbacks of the living Chloe with her dead husband likely to prove a popular ingredient in *Public Enemies*, so, regardless of their likelihood of advancing the investigation, the scenes would definitely be shown.

A couple of run-throughs and Chloe and Charles were set to go. Then suddenly the heavens opened. Geoffrey Ramage quickly decided they'd delay shooting until the cloudburst had passed. Much as his *film noir* instincts were drawn to dark moody shots through the falling rain, he knew that it hadn't been raining on the evening Martin Earnshaw really left, and it was his brief to reconstruct those events as closely as possible. The director comforted himself with the thought that, after the rain had stopped, he'd still be able to get some pretty damned dramatic effects with light reflecting off the wet pavement.

As the WET crew busied themselves covering their equipment against the downpour, Charles found himself invited into the house by Chloe Earnshaw. She led him through to a spotless kitchen and offered tea. Just as she was filling the kettle, the telephone rang. Chloe did nothing and after a moment the ringing stopped.

'Ansafone,' she replied to Charles's quizzical look. 'Get lots of calls – most of them from cranks.'

'Couldn't you change the number?'

She looked at him, appalled. 'No! All right, most of them are nonsense, but one of them might be important. One of them might be able to give me some information about Martin.'

'Yes, I'm sorry. Wasn't thinking.'

'It's all right.' She stared searchingly into his face and Charles felt himself transfixed by the intense beam of her dark blue eyes. 'You do look like him,' Chloe Earnshaw murmured. 'Not really like him, but there's something . . .'

'Ah. Well, sorry . . .' said Charles lamely.

'Not your fault. And indeed, if your likeness to Martin leads to us getting more information about the murder, then it will have been a very good thing – certainly nothing to apologize for.'

'No.' Still her eyes bored into him, making Charles uneasy. 'It must be awful for you,' he stumbled on, 'just sitting waiting for something to happen, having nothing to do.'

'Nothing to do?' she echoed incredulously. 'But I'm unbelievably busy.'

'Yes, of course you've got the house to look after and—'

'No, not that. I'm busy setting up this support group.'

'Support group – what for?'

'I'm setting up a national support group for the spouses and partners of murder victims,' Chloe Earnshaw replied sedately.

Well, yes, you *would* be, wouldn't you? Even as he had the thought, Charles knew it was yet another unworthy one.

After the filming, Charles changed out of his Martin Earnshaw kit and handed it over to the pretty Wardrobe girl. 'Anyone going out for a meal this evening?' he asked hopefully.

'Well, um . . .' The girl blushed. 'I'm not sure. I mean, I'm kind of committed.'

Geoffrey Ramage appeared in the doorway behind her and Charles instantly understood the nature of her commitment. The director, given overnight freedom from wife and small family, was going to make the most of it. Judging from the eye contact between him and the Wardrobe girl, it was a set-up job. He'd probably fixed for her to be allocated this particular duty. Some television traditions, like extramarital screwing on location, die hard.

'Oh, fine. Well, probably see you back at the hotel.'

'In the morning, Charles,' said Geoffrey Ramage firmly, emphasizing the exclusivity of his and the girl's plans for the evening.

Charles felt a momentary pang of wistfulness – even jealousy – in the car back to the hotel. He thought back to previous location filmings, when he'd set up similar arrangements for himself. In retrospect, none of them had been particularly successful. Indeed, given how rare it was for one to be successful, he wondered why the image of a one-night stand still retained any magic at all.

Charles Paris looked back gloomily on his sex life. There had been some wonderful moments, delirious, peaceful moments of pure pleasure, but their memory was hard to recapture. Something so perfect at the time does not make for good recollection, particularly when recollected in less cheerful mood. Thinking about such moments in the past only prompts mourning for their current absence.

Anyway, sexual highs never last. It's only the continuing relationships that count, he thought morbidly, picking at the scab of his self-pity. Awareness of his cooling relationship with Frances ached like a bruised bone.

There was a message for him back at the hotel. From Louise Denning. 'POSSIBILITY OF FURTHER FILMING TOMORROW (WED-

NESDAY). STAY AT HOTEL UNTIL CONTACTED.' She managed to get the same peremptory tone into all her communications.

Oh well, might mean another fee, thought Charles Paris morosely, as he ambled through into the bar.

A small Brighton hotel in late November is not likely to be doing much business, and there was only one other person drinking. A substantial figure sat hunched over the counter with his back to the door. Geoffrey Ramage was off with his quarry for some restaurant foreplay – or maybe they had gone straight up to the bedroom. And the rest of the WET crew were probably off bitching at everyone else in the business and milking their expenses over a rowdy Italian meal. I suppose I should eat something at some point, Charles reminded himself. Still, couple of large Bell's first.

As he approached the counter, he recognized the other drinker. It was Greg Marchmont, who gave him a deterrent sideways look and returned studiously to his whisky. The bleared look in his eye suggested it wasn't the first of the evening.

The bar was unmanned. Charles's repeated banging at the bell on the counter eventually produced a spotty waiter in a red jacket.

'Large Bell's, please.' And, in spite of the resolutely turned back, he added, 'Get you something, Sergeant?'

Marchmont turned to look at him and, after a moment's hesitation, said, 'I'll have the same, please.'

He took his drink with a murmured 'Thank you', and the spotty waiter left them to it. Doesn't look like being the most convivial evening since records began, thought Charles.

Still, better make some conversational effort. 'Your boss not around then, Sergeant?'

Greg Marchmont looked at him appraisingly, as if undecided whether or not to respond. Charles Paris had seen that look

83

many times before, and always from people who knew nothing about the theatre. It was what he thought of as the 'all actors are poofs' reaction.

But basic good manners just about triumphed. 'No, God knows where he is. Maybe he's found some Masonic function to go to down here.'

The detective sergeant remained surly and didn't volunteer anything else. If the conversation was to be maintained, Charles would have to be the one to keep it going.

'He seemed pretty sure of finding the murderer, didn't he? You know, when he was talking in the car . . . Sounded very confident.'

'Wankers always sound confident,' Marchmont growled. 'Goes with the territory.'

So his apparent deference to Roscoe only lasted while his superior was actually there. With the superintendent off the scene, Greg Marchmont showed as little respect as the rest of his colleagues.

'And is Roscoe a complete wanker?' asked Charles.

Marchmont gave a bitter laugh. 'You better believe it. One of those people who gets promoted for all the wrong reasons. Never done a single thing on his own, but always happy to take the credit for what his staff have done. He's a bloody joke throughout the force.'

'That's virtually what Ted Faraday said, wasn't it?'

'It's what anyone'd say.'

Since the subject had been raised, Charles couldn't resist a supplementary question. 'Why did Faraday actually leave the police? He implied it was because of some run-in with Roscoe . . . ?'

Greg Marchmont gave him another appraising look, and Charles knew that this was a significant one. The detective sergeant was deciding whether to pull out now or to settle in for an evening's drinking with an actor.

At the end of a long silence, Marchmont's gaze shifted to their glasses, which were both empty. 'Same again?'

Charles nodded. Greg Marchmont banged down on the bell. When they were resupplied with Bell's, Charles got his question answered. 'Ted Faraday was always an unconventional operator – tended to have a lot of criminal contacts and sailed pretty close to the wind a lot of the time. Coppers who work that way do sometimes set themselves up.'

'You mean, by getting too close to the criminals they're investigating?'

Marchmont nodded. 'Right. You want something from them, they usually want something from you. So often there's a trade-off for information.'

'What kind of trade-off? Money?'

'Not usually. No, a villain'll tell you what you want to know in return for . . . well, it can be a straight exchange of information. He tells us about some job one of his mates is planning, we tell him how much we know about what he's up to. Or maybe we agree to turn a blind eye to his next little effort . . . All kinds of different deals get done.'

'You need them as much as they need you.'

'Oh yes. But sometimes it goes a bit too far . . .'

'In what way?'

'Well, starts with a trade-off for information. I tell you this, says the villain – in return you don't shop me for that. Only a small step then for the villain to say – you don't shop me for that . . . in return for *this*. . . and he bungs the copper a few hundred.'

'Is that what happened with Faraday?'

The detective shrugged again. 'Don't know for sure. But he was well on the way to it. He was investigating a loan-sharking operation, and getting bloody close to the villains who were running it. OK, in order to get that close, he had to pretend he was on their side, he had to look like he was bent . . . Maybe that's all he was doing. Certainly that's all he *said* he was doing.'

'But he might actually have been bent?'

'There was evidence which could have suggested that. Certainly enough evidence for Roscoe to get him out of the force so quickly his feet didn't touch the ground.'

'But there were no actual charges against him?'

'No. Not enough evidence for that. I mean, opinion's divided. *I* reckon Faraday was straight and still is, but Roscoe'd wanted him out for years and saw his chance. Ted never made any secret of his opinion of our beloved superintendent.'

'Whereas you do . . .'

'What do you mean?' Marchmont demanded aggressively.

'Well, I've noticed you show a lot of respect to Roscoe when you're with him.'

The detective sergeant looked sullen. 'Yes, well, I can't afford to lose my job. Can't see me setting up as a PI somehow.'

They drank on. The idea of getting something to eat faded from Charles's mind. At midnight the spotty waiter said he was going to have to close the bar. They went up to Charles's room, where, inevitably, he had a half-full bottle of Bell's.

The room was bleak and impersonal. Charles tried to put from his mind all the other anonymous hotel rooms where he'd sat up too late drinking too much with people he hardly knew.

The remains of the bottle didn't last long. 'I'll order another from room service,' Charles announced when it was finished.

'All right,' said Marchmont, 'but I'm afraid it'll have to be on you. I'm bloody strapped for cash at the moment – shouldn't really have spent all that in the bar – so, sorry, if you get a bottle, I won't be able to return the favour – particularly knowing how much over the odds you usually pay for room service.'

'Don't worry,' said Charles with the magnanimity of the very drunk, 'I'm actually in work at the moment. I'll be happy to pay.'

'You get a good screw then, being an actor, do you?'

'Oh yes,' Charles lied.

The room-service bottle arrived – fortunately without notification of how much it was costing. That little surprise would be kept until Charles settled his bill.

The two men recharged their glasses and Greg Marchmont expanded on his financial problems. 'It's the bloody maintenance that kills. God, I should never have got into that divorce.'

'Any kids?' asked Charles.

'Three of the little buggers. God, with what I have to pay for them and for her, I've hardly got a bloody penny to call my own. You divorced?'

'No,' Charles replied, wondering lugubriously how long he would be able to give that answer.

'Keep it that way if you don't want to be ruined for life.'

'Have you remarried?'

Marchmont shook his head. 'No, I've managed to end up with the worst of all worlds. Broke up my marriage to go off with someone else, then as soon as the divorce is all sorted out and definite, she pisses off and leaves me.'

'Ah. It is supposed to put a lot of strain on marriages, isn't it? Police work, I mean. Like the theatre, actually.'

'Hm. Well, I don't know if you can blame the police. I just met someone else and fell for her hook, line and bloody sinker.'

'Someone else in the force?'

'Oh yes.' Marchmont's glazed eyes focused on Charles for a moment. 'You've met her actually.'

He knew immediately who it was. 'Sam? Sam Noakes?'

A mournful nod confirmed it. 'Uh-huh. And now she's every telly viewer's favourite bloody wank.'

'Her and Chloe Earnshaw.'

'Hm. Yes, I wouldn't mind giving her one either.' The detective looked dejectedly down into his dwindling drink. 'Sodding women – why do we bother with them? Only leads to bloody heartbreak.'

'Why did Sam leave you?' asked Charles gently.

'Why? Because I wasn't good enough for her, I guess. I was just a DS and didn't show much sign of ever getting above that.'

'So you weren't rich enough?'

'It's not money with her, no. Sam's a control freak. She likes to feel she's in charge. Sex for her is just another way of demonstrating her power. She wanted to prove she was powerful enough to break up my marriage and I guess when she'd done that, I ceased to be a challenge for her, so she moved on. It's the same with her career – she's very single-minded.'

'And good, isn't she?'

'Oh yes, bloody good. Way out of my league. She was same intake as me, actually – came first in the class at everything. No, she can go right to the top.'

'And wants to?'

'You bet. You wouldn't begin to believe that woman's ambition. I used to think she was joking, some of the things she said she wanted to achieve, but now I know it's all for real. It'd give her a bloody orgasm to be first woman Commissioner of Scotland Yard.'

'Regardless of who gets trampled on the way . . . ?'

'Yup.' Tears welled up in the detective's eyes. 'Wish I'd never met the cow. Should've stayed with Maureen and the kids. Now I've lost them, I'm permanently bloody broke, I'm put under intolerable pressure to do a whole load of stuff I don't want to do, I'm—'

'What kind of stuff?'

'Oh, nothing. Doesn't matter.'

'And what do you feel for Sam now?' There was a silence. 'I mean, if she'd have you back, what would you—?'

'Oh, I'd jump. Like a bloody rabbit. Straight back for more humiliation. When you've had a woman like that . . . you're ruined. I'm still totally obsessed with her. Do anything she asks me, even if . . .' Marchmont sighed. 'I'm just totally fucked up.'

He brushed the back of his hand savagely against his face. 'Come on, pour us another one.'

Charles half filled the glass and the detective downed its contents in one angry swallow.

'When Sam walked out on you . . .' Charles began tentatively, 'did she walk straight in with someone else?'

'Oh yes,' Marchmont replied bitterly. 'As if I needed it bloody rubbed in.'

'Who did she move in with?' asked Charles, feeling pretty certain he knew the answer.

He was right. 'Ted bloody Faraday,' said Greg Marchmont.

Chapter Nine

Charles's hangover the next morning felt like he'd had a face-lift without benefit of anaesthetic. It was as if all the skin had been scoured back and twisted into a little knot of pain at the point where his spine met his skull. So tight had it been pulled that it compressed the brain agonizingly inside his cranium. His head had to be kept at a constant level and moved infinitely gently, like a conjuror's magic ball supported on the edge of a scarf.

The knowledge that DS Greg Marchmont ought to be feeling at least as bad was small comfort. Probably he wasn't, anyway. No doubt a whisky session like that was routine for a hard-bitten copper.

There were certain kill-or-cure options available to Charles, one of which – readily available in a hotel – was a Full English Breakfast. If he could actually get that down him, he knew it would ultimately help. But the dry nausea in his throat cast doubt on whether he could manage that pivotal first mouthful without throwing up.

So he just lay prone, sticky under the sheets, hoping for a blessed return to sleep. He'd woken at five, and deep down he knew that was it for the night. Maybe get a zizz in the afternoon if he had a few drinks at lunchtime.

That was of course another kill-or-cure option – the old 'hair of the dog'. And it was an option that he had been resorting to too often recently. Charles felt grimly virtuous that he and Marchmont had drained the previous night's bottle to its last bead of condensation. Otherwise he knew he'd have been straight at it again.

Anyway, he needed to sober up, not extend the binge. He was, after all, potentially working that day. Although impersonating Martin Earnshaw was not the most complex role he'd ever attempted, playing the dead man drunk might have led to serious misidentifications from the viewing public. And one of Charles Paris's residual professional rules was not to get pissed when he was working. Well, try not to.

The thought of work prompted him to attempt getting up. Further instructions about the day's filming, Charles told himself, might be waiting at Reception. Of course he knew that if WET really needed him they would have rung through to his room, but he did need some motivation for the potentially hazardous transition from horizontal to vertical.

It took him about an hour and it wasn't easy. Shaving was the real killer. He finished with half a dozen cuts, his head looking, he reflected ghoulishly, rather too much like Martin Earnshaw's might when it was finally discovered. Still, if he was required for filming that day, Make-Up could no doubt patch him up.

It was after half past ten when he got downstairs and they'd stopped serving breakfast; at least he was spared the decision about that option. There was no message for him at Reception, so presumably he'd just have to wait around the hotel until he heard something.

Charles moved through to the lounge and ordered a pot of coffee. He'd try to be strong and put off the first drink of the day as long as possible. The coffee scalded his tongue and he sat there in miserable isolation with the mortifying knowledge that he could blame no one but himself for his condition.

There was no sign of his drinking partner. Greg Marchmont had probably been on duty first thing in the morning, shaking off the night's alcohol like the hard man he was. Oh God, thought Charles, nourishing his self-pity, I can't even hold my liquor like other men.

The couple who came and joined him did little to lift his

mood. Geoffrey Ramage and his Wardrobe girl were glowing from the effects of a major sexual work-out. The director exuded the satisfaction of proved masculinity. This was all Charles needed.

He did, however, have a small moment of revenge. Geoffrey and the girl were going through a rather coy farewell routine, about how she was going back to London on the train and how he was driving, and how wonderful it had been and how they'd hope to meet up again soon, when Charles said, 'Oh, hadn't you heard – we might be wanted for more filming today?'

'What?' Geoffrey Ramage looked shocked.

'Had a message last night. More information from the public, I imagine. They may want us to do another reconstruction.'

'Oh,' said the director.

The Wardrobe girl insinuated her hand into his. 'Might mean we have to do another overnight,' she purred.

'Yes,' said Geoffrey; and then, justifiably afraid that the word hadn't sounded very enthusiastic, repeated assertively, '*Yes*.'

But his face was a picture, and Charles Paris couldn't help being amused by it. The director was in his late forties. He'd just given his all in a night of sexual passion, secure in the knowledge that, after fond farewells to his bit on the side, he could go home and sleep it off. Now suddenly the spectre had arisen of having to do a repeat performance.

Lunchtime arrived, and there was still no word from WET. Geoffrey Ramage went to phone Roger Parkes and came back with the news that no decision had yet been made. They were to wait in the hotel for further instructions. But if there was more filming to be done, it would definitely be after dark again.

'Ooh,' the Wardrobe girl giggled. 'Sounds promising.'

Geoffrey Ramage curbed his evident irritation and smiled feebly at her. They all went through to the bar.

The eternal but regrettable fact of life was once again proved true – another drink did make Charles feel unbelievably better. Large Bell's to jump-start the system, followed by a pint of beer to irrigate it. The idea of living another day no longer seemed inconceivable.

After a couple, they were joined in the bar by Roscoe and Marchmont. The superintendent's ghastly leisurewear and bonhomous mood were once again in evidence, but the sergeant still seemed edgy in his superior's presence. Marchmont looked rather the worse for wear, but made no reference to the previous evening, perhaps ashamed of having given so much of himself away to a comparative stranger.

Roscoe decided they'd go through to the dining room to eat. Geoffrey Ramage moved to join them.

'But, Geoff,' whispered the Wardrobe girl, 'weren't we going to eat on our own?'

'No, no. No need to be antisocial,' the director replied breezily.

The Wardrobe girl gave him a sour look as they moved through. Greg Marchmont lingered at the bar.

'Aren't you joining us?' asked Roscoe.

'No. Don't need a full meal, just a snack. Not a big eater at lunchtime.'

'Come on, come on, don't worry about the old exes. This one's on me, Greg.'

Reluctantly, but unable to refuse, the sergeant followed his superior through into the dining room.

It wasn't the most convivial meal of all time. As Geoffrey Ramage responded less and less to her innuendoes, the atmosphere between him and the Wardrobe girl became distinctly frosty. Marchmont, cowed by Roscoe's presence or perhaps embarrassed by Charles's, was monosyllabic. Only the superintendent and the actor showed signs of animation. In Charles this was prompted by the simple blessed fact of feeling human again; what lay behind Roscoe's good humour he had no way of knowing; but the two of them certainly did most of the talking.

In their conversation Charles was quite content to take the role of feed. Roscoe liked nothing better than expatiating on his work and how skilful he was at it, so Charles obligingly prompted pontification and reminiscence.

'What always matters . . . in police work . . . anywhere,' the superintendent announced at one point, 'is having the right person in charge. Leadership is what counts. If you've got the right person directing the skills of others, co-ordinating their talents, then you're going to end up with an efficient operation.'

There was no doubt, from the way he spoke, that Roscoe regarded himself as 'the right person'.

'Are you actually in charge of the Earnshaw case?' Charles asked obediently.

'Well, of course, there's a chain of command, and mine is really no more than a watching brief, but—' The Superintendent winked knowingly '—let's say not a lot happens on the case that I don't know about . . .'

Once again, as it had in the car, this boastfulness seemed to make Marchmont uncomfortable. And once again Charles reflected how much less easy a ride Roscoe would be having were any of his other subordinates present. What was the hold the superintendent had over the detective sergeant?

'And I think you said the whole television involvement in the case was your idea?' Charles prompted.

'Oh yes. You see, I recognized from the start that in this case we were up against a criminal of exceptional cunning and intelligence . . .'

This was patent nonsense. When the case first arose and *Public Enemies* first became involved, there was not even a definite crime to solve. To speak of profiling the criminal at that point was ridiculous. Still, Charles, blissfully marinating in more restorative beer, was content to let the self-congratulation ramble on.

'. . . so I thought the more resources there were pitched against him, the better. Television, the best brains at Scotland Yard, everything . . . any criminal who could remain undetected by all that lot was clearly going to be something rather special.'

'But he *has* actually remained undetected by all that lot, hasn't he?' said Charles, introducing the first contentious note into the conversation.

Superintendent Roscoe was unruffled. He smiled benificently. 'So it might appear, but don't worry, everything's in hand.'

'And you think it'll be the police who get him?'

'As opposed to who?'

'As opposed to Ted Faraday.' A shadow passed over Roscoe's face at the name. 'I mean, that challenge was put out on *Public Enemies* by Bob Garston, wasn't it? Did you approve of that happening?'

'Well, I wasn't sure that . . .' The superintendent recovered himself. 'Yes, of course I approved of it. Nothing goes on that programme without my say-so.'

'So do you think Faraday's in with a chance of finding out anything useful?'

'Not a snowball's chance in hell,' Roscoe replied complacently.

Charles remembered the fax he'd seen in the *Public Enemies* outer office. 'But he's still reporting in to WET. He says he's gone underground here in Brighton and—'

The superintendent's voice was heavy with contempt. 'Ted Faraday's idea of going underground is about as subtle as that of an ostrich. We know exactly where he's hidden himself, don't we, Greg?' Marchmont looked more uncomfortable than ever at this appeal for corroboration. 'If hiding yourself in a rented flat in Trafalgar Lane is going underground—' The irony grew ever weightier '—then he's certainly managed to vanish off the face of the earth. And what a master of disguise he is! No one in the entire country has recognized him, *I'm sure.*'

'So I gather you don't think he's likely to solve the case?'

Superintendent Roscoe laughed heartily. 'I don't know if you're a betting man, Mr Paris . . .'

'Very occasionally.'

'Well, I will bet you any money you care to mention that Ted Faraday will not contribute in any way to the solving of this case.'

They'd reached the end of the meal. Charles Paris felt welcome waves of drowsiness wash over him. He yawned. 'I'm totally wasted. Let me know if there's any summons from WET. I'm going up to my bed for an hour.'

'Ooh, there's a thought,' said the Wardrobe girl winsomely.

Geoffrey Ramage's face was a study.

It was dark when Charles woke. His head still throbbed and he felt pretty grisly, but he knew it was a grisliness which would evaporate in half an hour, leaving him restored. Must watch the booze tonight, though, he thought. Don't want to start the whole cycle up again. In fact, really, I shouldn't have another drink today. No, I won't. Well, I'll try not to.

He looked at his watch. After five. Surely there wouldn't be anything from WET so late. And somebody would have rung through to him if he had been needed.

He looked down at the telephone and, on an impulse, rang Frances's number.

'Hello?' Her voice sounded furry, as thought he had woken her.

'Hi. It's me. Charles.'

'Oh.' A silence. 'Any particular reason?'

'No, I just, er . . . I was in Brighton and I was, er, at a loose end . . .'

'Oh, *thanks.*'

96

'Sorry, I didn't mean . . .'

'It's all right. So what are you doing in Brighton – a dandruff commercial?'

'No, no. Well, you're close. Another of these reconstruction things.'

'Ah.'

'You know he's definitely dead, don't you? And I'm now playing the part of a murder victim.'

'I do read the papers, Charles.'

'Yes. Yes, of course. You getting any reflected glory? People at school saying, "Ooh, I saw your husband on telly last night, doing his well-known impression of a dismembered corpse"?'

'I don't think anyone at school knows you're my husband. Half of them don't even know I've *got* a husband. Anyway, I haven't been in school for the last few days.'

A sudden icicle stabbed at Charles's heart. 'You are all right, are you, Frances?'

'Yes, yes. I've just been getting overtired recently. Touch of flu. Lot of it about this time of year.'

'Mm.' A little silence. 'You're sure that there's nothing—?'

'Charles, Charles, I've got *a touch of flu.*'

'Yes, OK.'

'You're keeping well, are you?'

'Well . . . Rather hungover this morning, I'm afraid.'

'So what else is new?'

Their conversation dwindled into platitudes and soon ended. Charles felt shaken as he put the phone down. Yes, of course she'd just got flu. This time. But one time it wouldn't just be flu and . . . They were neither of them getting any younger. He was shocked by how much the thought upset him.

He needed fresh air. On his way out he asked at Reception whether there had been any message for him.

'What name was it?' the adenoidal girl asked.

'Paris. Charles Paris.' She shook her head. 'I'm with the WET lot.'

'What, for the filming?'

'Yes.'

'Ooh, there was a message about that.'

'What? Was it on? Have they gone off to the location?'

'Erm . . .' With infuriating slowness the girl shuffled through a pile of message slips. 'Here we are. Message from WET . . .'

'Yes?'

'From the *Public Enemies* office.'

'Yes . . . ?'

'That's that one with Bob Garston, isn't it? I like that. It's the one where—'

'Yes, what was the message?'

''Ere, you've been on that, haven't you? You're the bloke what got killed down here.'

'Well, I play the part of that man in the reconstructions, but I'm not—'

'Fancy that. How spooky.'

'What was the bloody message!'

'All right, all right, keep your hair on.' She consulted the slip. '"NO MORE FILMING. RETURN TO LONDON."'

'And the rest of the crew have all gone?'

'Checked out over two hours ago.'

'And no one thought to pass the news on to me?'

'No.'

The girl had clearly taken a Louise Denning Correspondence Course in Tact and Diplomacy.

'What about the police – Roscoe and Marchmont – have they gone too?'

'Those gentlemen are still booked in.'

Charles asked whether his room was booked for another night and heard with no surprise that it wasn't. 'So I just have to pack my bags and go, is that it?'

'That's it . . .' the girl assured him cheerfully, as she produced a printed bill, '. . . just as soon as you've settled *this*.'

And Charles Paris discovered how much a room-service bottle of whisky really cost. It was not a happy discovery.

He was walking disconsolately up towards the station when the headlights of a passing car illuminated a familiar figure some fifty yards away. It was Greg Marchmont, shoulders hunched, looking neither to left nor right and moving purposefully ahead. Charles could easily have caught up, but instead some instinct made him moderate his pace and trail the detective.

It seemed for a while that their destination was the same, as Marchmont strode along Queen's Road. But when he got close to Brighton Station he veered off down the steep tunnel towards the car park entrance. Charles followed, noting with interest that they were in Trafalgar Road.

Greg Marchmont suddenly turned right and, as Charles did the same, he looked up at the street name. Without surprise he registered that it was Trafalgar Lane.

The detective moved steadily forward through the dim lighting, apparently unsuspicious that he might be being followed. He stopped outside a second-hand clothes shop, whose dusty window suggested that it had long since ceased trading. Charles, who had kept a constant fifty yards between them since first spotting his quarry, slid into a doorway and watched.

Marchmont looked up at the shop's first-floor window, from which a little light spilled through a crack in the curtains. He checked his watch and stood for a moment undecided. Then, seeing the lights of a pub a little way down the road, he set off towards it.

When Marchmont entered the pub, Charles was about level with the second-hand clothes shop. The actor took in the broken bell-push beside a side door, which presumably led to the flat over the shop. Light still showed from the window above.

He hesitated for a moment, before following his quarry into the pub. He wasn't quite sure what he was doing, or why he was doing it, but felt he was getting close to something significant. The coincidence of Greg Marchmont going to Trafalgar Lane had to have some connection with Ted Faraday.

The pub was scruffy, with fruit machines and Country music blaring from the jukebox. As he entered Charles saw the back view of Greg Marchmont at the bar ordering a drink. That should keep you in here for a little while, he thought, and give me time to investigate the flat up the road.

There was another reason for getting out. As soon as he'd entered the pub, Charles had found himself facing a short, bespectacled grey-haired man, wearing a neat raincoat and nursing a half-pint of lager. The expression of affront and positive hostility which his arrival brought to the man's face decided Charles to leave the pub as soon as possible.

Outside again, he wasn't certain what to do next. So, maybe he had discovered where Ted Faraday had gone undercover in Brighton . . . so what? The private investigator wasn't breaking any laws. What he was doing was not Charles Paris's business. In fact, the best thing Charles could do would be to walk back to the station and catch the next train to London.

But, even as he reached this decision, the light above the second-hand clothes shop went out. Charles pressed back into the shadows and watched.

Sure enough, after a few seconds, the door beside the shop-front opened, and a tramplike figure emerged, swaddled in layers of grubby overcoat, with a large woolly hat pulled down over straggly hair. The face was hidden by a ragged scarf.

The tramp was carrying a large package about three feet long, wrapped in dirty opaque polythene and tied with string.

He locked the door, glanced both ways up the street, and set off in the direction of the station. Charles followed.

There was something strange about the way the man moved.

A slight limp, but not a regular limp. The sort of limp in fact that would be used by someone unused to limping.

With a little leap of excitement, the actor in Charles Paris recognized what it was. The walk of someone putting on a limp. The man ahead of him was in disguise.

Ted Faraday's ironic words from the WET hospitality suite came back to him. 'I am a master of disguise.'

The tramp seemed deliberately to be taking an erratic course. At the end of Trafalgar Lane, he turned left and left again to walk along the parallel Kemp Street. When this met Gloucester Road, he maintained the zigzag, doubling back down Over Road. It was as if he was trying to confuse any potential pursuer, and yet nothing in his behaviour had indicated he knew that he really was being followed.

Charles's mind seethed with possibilities – particularly about the contents of the package. It was clearly heavy, because the tramp kept shifting its weight from shoulder to shoulder.

Charles Paris was concentrating so much on what lay ahead of him that he did not think to look behind. He was only aware of his assailant when his arms were suddenly pinioned.

'You are under arrest,' announced a voice, very close in his ear.

'What!' Charles twisted round in the iron grip sufficiently to see the face of the bespectacled man from the pub. 'What did you say?'

'This is a citizen's arrest,' said the man in his weedy, jobs-worth's voice.

'Do me a favour!' Charles turned back to see the tramp disappearing out of sight at the end of the road. 'What on earth do you think you're arresting me for?'

'Because I recognized you,' said the little man self-righteously. 'I've seen you on the telly. You are Martin Earnshaw and I'm arresting you on a charge of wasting police time by pretending you've been murdered.'

'Oh, for God's sake!' said Charles Paris.

Chapter Ten

The little man had got a firm lock on Charles and proved to be surprisingly strong. 'I used to be in the Commandos,' his voice hissed. 'I know about immobilizing an enemy. So don't you try anything. You won't get away from me.'

'Oh, for heaven's sake!' said Charles. 'This is ridiculous. I don't want to get into a fight. I am *not* Martin Earnshaw.'

'Well, you look like him.'

'Yes, I do look like him. That is the whole point. I am an actor and I got the job of playing Martin Earnshaw in the *Public Enemies* reconstruction for the very simple reason that I *do* look like him.'

'A likely story,' the little man sneered.

'Oh, just let me go!'

Charles tried a sudden movement to jerk himself free, but the hold remained firm. Whether he'd learnt it in the Commandos or not, the little man certainly knew how to restrain a captive. Charles gave up struggling. 'So what are you proposing to do with me then?'

'I'm going to take you to the police station and turn you over to the proper authorities. I know my duty as a citizen,' the little man concluded piously.

'But look, I can *prove* I'm not Martin Earnshaw. My name is Charles Paris. I'm an actor. I have credit cards in my wallet to prove it.'

'You could have stolen those.'

'Why should I?'

'You might have wanted to disguise your identity, so that the police wouldn't get on to you.'

'Look, if I was Martin Earnshaw and was going to disguise my identity, I'd make a darned sight better job of it than this.'

'Ah, so you admit you *are* Martin Earnshaw.'

'No, I don't!' God, this was like arguing with a three-year-old. 'All I'm saying is, if I *was* Martin Earnshaw, I'd have disguised myself by making my face look different, wouldn't I, not just by stealing someone's bloody credit cards!'

'All criminals make that one little mistake,' the little man countered with infuriating complacency. 'And you might have got away with it . . . if you hadn't had the bad luck to come up against me.'

Who did he think he was, for God's sake – Superman?

'Look, could you just for one moment be sensible? Let go of me and I will *prove* to you that I'm not Martin Earnshaw. I mean, of course I'm not Martin Earnshaw! The man's dead, apart from anything else!'

'*Apparently* dead,' the little man riposted slyly.

'Oh . . . !' Charles made another attempt to break free. This time a sudden lurch sideways caught his captor off balance, and the two of them fell to the pavement. But the wiry arms kept their grip, still immobilizing Charles's own. He tried to roll them both over and use his weight to get the little man – literally – off his back.

It was in the course of this undignified scrabbling that he became aware of a tall figure leaning over them and a ponderous voice asking, 'What's going on here then?'

Charles Paris squinted up to see the outline of a uniformed constable. Never had the sight been more welcome. It carried all the nostalgic *Dixon of Dock Green* reassurance of the good old English bobby on the beat.

'Thank goodness you're here, officer. Would you please ask this gentleman to let me go?'

'Depends rather on the reasons why he grabbed hold of you in the first place, I'd have thought.'

'He got hold of me for all the wrong reasons. It's a case of mistaken identity.'

'Ah, so you admit it!' the little man's voice crowed gleefully from somewhere beneath Charles.

'What *is* going on here?' the constable asked wearily.

'I've just made a citizen's arrest.'

'Why? What for?'

'Wasting police time. This man is pretending he's someone else – and also pretending he's been murdered.'

'What? Come on, you'd better get up, both of you.'

They shambled to their feet. It wasn't easy, as the little man did not for a moment relax his hold. When they were upright, Charles asked politely, 'Could you ask him to let me go, please?'

'In a minute,' the policeman replied slowly. 'When we know what's what. Very good hold he's got on you there, actually.'

Charles could almost feel the little man glow with pride behind him. 'Yes, well, I was in the Commandos, you know.'

'Really? My dad was in the Royal Signals – Desert War – flushing out Rommel and his—'

Charles was exasperated. 'Look, could we please defer the military reminiscences until I've been released.'

He knew as he spoke that his tone of voice was wrong, and the beady look the constable cast on him confirmed this. 'All right, all right. In my experience, people who make citizen's arrests usually do so for a very good reason. So let's get a few facts first, shall we?' In time-honoured fashion, the policeman drew out a notebook. 'Start with names, eh?'

'My name's Kevin Littlejohn,' said the ex-Commando.

Yes, it bloody would be, thought Charles.

'And yours?'

'My name is Charles Paris.'

'No, it isn't,' said Kevin Littlejohn. 'It's Martin Earnshaw.'

The constable reacted to the name and looked closely into Charles's face. 'Yes, you certainly look like him.'

'I *know* I look like him. That is the whole reason why—'

Apparently unaware that he was speaking exclusively in clichés, the policeman announced heavily, 'I think you'd better come along to the station with me, sir.'

'Look, this is *ridiculous!*' Charles repeated yet again to the desk sergeant. 'My name is Charles Paris, not Martin Earnshaw!'

'You look very like Martin Earnshaw,' said the sergeant suspiciously.

'Yes, of course I look like him. How many more times do I have to say this? I am being employed to look like him. The sole reason I was given the job was *because* I look like him!'

'I don't think this bolshie attitude is helping your cause very much, Mr Earnshaw.'

'I am *not* Mr Earnshaw! I am an actor called Charles Paris!'

'Really?' The desk sergeant looked sceptical. 'I've never heard of you.'

'No, all right. Well, maybe I'm that sort of actor. The profession is crowded with actors you've probably never heard of. I mean, I dare say you watch a bit of television, but do you ever go to the theatre?'

'Your tone is getting somewhat offensive, Mr Earnshaw.'

'For the last time, I am *not* Mr Earnshaw!'

The desk sergeant tutted. 'When I think of that poor wife of yours ... What you've put her through ... it's ... well, it's just unbelievable.'

'You know nothing about my wife.'

'Yes, I do. I've seen her on the telly. And you've allowed that poor young woman to believe that you've been murdered and all the time you've been hiding away—'

'I have not. Chloe Earnshaw has nothing to do with me.'

'I don't blame her,' Kevin Littlejohn opined righteously. 'After the way you've treated her.'

God, it was exasperating. The constable who'd brought him

into the station had gone back on the beat, but the desk sergeant demonstrated exactly the same bovine incomprehension. And the presence of Kevin Littlejohn didn't help. The little ex-Commando sat, blinking excitedly behind his spectacles, watching every detail of the interview. This was the most exciting thing that had happened to him since the disappointment of the Second World War ending.

The desk sergeant tried a more conciliatory approach. 'Do you have any proof that you are who you claim to be, Mr Earnshaw?'

Charles managed to restrain himself from reacting to the name this time, and said, through clenched teeth, 'I have shown you my wallet. You have seen the credit cards in the name of "Charles Paris". What other proof do you need?'

'You could have stolen those,' Kevin Littlejohn repeated.

'Yes, you could have stolen those,' the desk sergeant agreed.

'Well, what *do* you want then?'

'We just want someone who can vouch for you, who can prove you're who you say you are.'

'There are thousands of people who can do that!'

'Like who?'

As ever in such circumstances, Charles's mind went a complete blank. 'Well . . . well . . . Chloe Earnshaw!' he announced dramatically.

'Chloe Earnshaw? Your wife?'

'No. *Not* my wife—that is the whole point! Chloe Earnshaw could take one look at me and tell you categorically that I am not her husband.'

The desk sergeant looked dubious. 'I don't know . . . I think you've caused her enough suffering already. It'd have to be broken to her very gently that you were actually alive after all this time.'

Charles groaned in frustration. 'Look, can't you get it into your thick skull that—?'

'That is no way to speak to a police officer,' said the desk sergeant, affronted.

'No, it's no way to speak to a police officer,' Kevin Littlejohn echoed. 'In my young day people had respect for authority. That sort of talk wouldn't have been tolerated in the Commandos. We wouldn't have won the war if people had been allowed to talk like that, would we?'

'No,' the desk sergeant agreed.

Suddenly Charles saw a route through this thicket of mis-understanding. Very calmly, he said, 'I'm sorry. I didn't mean to be offensive. But I've just thought of someone who can vouch for who I am. He is someone who is actually here in Brighton at the moment, and he's a senior police officer.'

'Oh yes?' The desk sergeant sounded sceptical. 'Who is he?'

'His name is Superintendent Roscoe. He is in charge of – or at least connected with – the Martin Earnshaw murder case.'

'If it *is* a murder case,' Kevin Littlejohn interposed doubtfully.

Charles managed to curb his reaction to this, and continued evenly, 'Superintendent Roscoe is staying at the hotel I've been staying at for the last couple of days. If you ring him there, I'm sure he will be able to tell you who I am.'

The desk sergeant still wasn't totally convinced, but Roscoe's name had struck some chord and he was prepared at least to call Charles's bluff. 'What's the name of the hotel?' he asked.

He rang through and it was confirmed that Superintendent Roscoe was staying there.

'See,' said Charles, 'see! How would I have known that if I wasn't down here for the filming as I said I was?'

While the hotel receptionist tried to make contact with Super-intendent Roscoe's room, the desk sergeant gave Charles a nar-row look over the receiver. 'It is not unknown for criminals of a certain exhibitionist type to follow closely the police investi-gations into the crimes in which they are implicated.'

Charles threw his eyes to heaven. The desk sergeant reacted

to something said at the other end and put the phone down. 'He's not there.'

'Well, ring them back and give them a message for him to ring here as soon as he gets in!'

'Don't you order me around, Mr Earnshaw.'

'For the last bloody time, I am *not* Mr Earnshaw!' Charles's anger was by now almost uncontrollable. 'Listen, is it impossible for your single brain cell to cope with the idea that you might be wrong?'

'Don't you be offensive, Mr Earnshaw!'

'No, don't you be offensive!' Kevin Littlejohn parroted.

'Don't you start! I don't care whether you used to be in the Commandos or not, you're now nothing but an officious little nit-picker!'

The desk sergeant came immediately to Littlejohn's defence. 'There's no need to insult someone just because he has a sense of civic duty. Let me tell you, if more people shared Mr Littlejohn's attitude to responsibility, our job would be a lot easier. It's malicious time-wasters like you, Mr Earnshaw, who cause the trouble!'

It was a long time since Charles Paris had been so angry. Maybe the sour, aching residue of his hangover shortened his temper, or maybe it was just the mindless self-righteousness of the two men he was up against that got him going. Whatever the cause, Charles, normally a man to avoid confrontation, found himself shouting back, almost totally out of control. 'I have never encountered such incredible stupidity! All right, anyone can make a mistake, but now you should recognize it's a mistake and bloody let me go! Or can't your Neanderthal mind stretch to take that idea on board!!!'

There was a silence before the desk sergeant said, 'Neanderthal, eh?' Another silence. 'What's that mean then?'

The storm in Charles had blown itself out. 'Oh, never mind,' he sighed wearily.

'Neanderthal,' said Kevin Littlejohn smugly, 'means prehistoric or underdeveloped.'

'Oh, *does* it?' said the desk sergeant, his voice heavy with menace.

Charles Paris wasn't really surprised to be confined to a cell for the night. He submitted passively to the indignities of having his bag and pocket contents inventoried and his belt and shoe-laces removed. The desk sergeant assured him grimly that a message would be left at the hotel for Superintendent Roscoe, but Charles wasn't convinced.

Oh well, he thought, as he lay down on the thin mattress under the unforgiving nightlight, serves me bloody well right, doesn't it? Be a long time before I lose my temper again.

The only possible advantage of his situation was that he did – albeit inadvertently – achieve his wish of not having another drink that day.

Charles Paris didn't sleep much during his incarceration, and was quite encouraged to discover that what he missed most through the long watches of the night was not a bottle but a book. He really felt bereft without anything to read; that would be the abiding memory for him of the deprivations of prison life.

Breakfast in the morning was pretty dire and, in spite of Charles's questions, the policeman who brought it volunteered no information about what was going to happen to him. Surely they can't keep me long without charging me, thought Charles, trying desperately to remember what little he knew of the law. Wasn't there something called habeas corpus which guaranteed prisoners certain rights in these circumstances?

Yes, surely he'd been in a late episode of *Z Cars* where that had been a significant plot point. He scoured his memory for more detail, but the only thing that had stayed with him was the notice *Stage* had given of his performance. 'If real-life offenders were as ineffectual as Charles Paris's villain, then the battle against crime would be as good as won.'

That recollection didn't help much. Half formed beneath the surface of his mind lurked the anxiety that, however long they decided to keep him in the cell, there wasn't a lot he could do about it.

Relief came late morning when his door was opened by a taciturn constable who led him through into an office. There, to his surprise, Charles found Superintendent Roscoe, dressed in full uniform, sitting on his own behind a desk. The officer looked half amused and distinctly smug.

'Well then . . . what have you been getting up to, Mr Paris?'

'A misunderstanding. Some old idiot got convinced that I actually was Martin Earnshaw.'

'So I gather. Don't worry, that's been sorted out. They now know who you really are.'

'Oh. Thank you. And indeed thank you for coming here this morning. I'm sorry, I just couldn't think of anyone else whose name would have had the same effect.'

Roscoe inclined his head, accepting the implied compliment. 'But I understand it wasn't just a case of mistaken identity . . . ?'

'What do you mean?'

The superintendent looked down at some notes in front of him. 'Coppers don't like being insulted any more than the rest of the population. What did you reckon – that the desk sergeant wouldn't understand the word "Neanderthal"?'

'He didn't,' Charles couldn't help saying.

'No.' Roscoe examined the notes. 'Had a bit of a problem spelling it too.'

Charles chuckled, but the cold eyes that peered up at him told him the superintendent was not in joking mood. 'Insulting a police officer could be quite a serious charge, Mr Paris.'

'I was just frustrated by his stupidity. Surely it's not very serious?'

'We can generally speaking make a charge as serious or unserious as we choose to. Just as we can generally speaking make an investigation as detailed or perfunctory as we choose to. And on the whole you'll find the police tend to look after their own.'

Charles nodded, chastened.

'What I want to know, Mr Paris, is what you were doing round that part of Brighton last night anyway . . . ?'

'Well, I . . .'

'The message from WET that you weren't required for further filming got to the hotel early afternoon. I wonder why you didn't just take a train straight back to London then.'

'I was asleep.'

'Oh yes?'

'Nobody gave me the message.'

'Still doesn't explain what you were doing where you were found last night.' Charles was silent, undecided how much he should reveal. 'Mr Paris,' the superintendent went on, 'it's come to my notice, from sources which I have no intention of revealing, that you have occasionally in the past dabbled in a bit of crime investigation yourself . . .'

'Well . . .'

'If there's one thing a real policeman hates, Mr Paris, it's the idea of some bloody amateur muscling in on the act.'

'Yes. Right.'

'So please don't tell me your activities last night had anything to do with you trying to do a bit of investigation into the Martin Earnshaw case off your own bat.'

'No. No, that wasn't what I was doing. I'll tell you exactly what happened.'

And he did. He described how he'd caught sight of DS Marchmont and started following him 'just out of curiosity'; and he went right through to the moment when his trailing of the 'tramp' had been interrupted by Kevin Littlejohn's 'citizen's arrest'.

At the end of his narrative there was a silence before Superintendent Roscoe said, 'I see. And no doubt you have a theory about who the "tramp" was . . .'

'I think it was Ted Faraday in disguise.'

'Do you? And may I have the benefit of your theory about what he might have been carrying?'

'I hadn't really thought about that.'

'It seems to me there's quite a lot you "hadn't really thought about", Mr Paris.' Roscoe was angry now. 'Not least the potential chaos that could be caused by some unqualified amateur getting involved in a professional police investigation!'

'I'm sorry. I didn't mean—'

'I can see to it you're not charged for this lot, Mr Paris—' The Superintendent gestured to the desk '—but if I ever hear that you've been doing anything in this case other than the acting job for which WET are employing you—' A blunt finger was held in front of Charles's face '—I will see to it that you get put away for an uncomfortably long time. Got that?'

Charles Paris assured the superintendent that he had got that. How much longer the dressing-down might have gone on was hard to know, because he was let off the hook by the appearance of a uniformed constable at the office door. 'Urgent call for you, Superintendent. It's being switched through here.'

'Thanks.' The phone on the desk pinged and Roscoe picked it up. 'What? Where? Has it been cordoned off? Are the public being kept away? OK, I'll be right there.' He put the phone down and picked up his peaked cap. 'I must go.'

'Development on the Earnshaw case?' Charles couldn't help asking.

A stubby finger was again thrust very close to his nose. 'Have you not got the message yet, Mr Paris? Mind your own fucking business!'

Chapter Eleven

It was after one by the time Charles Paris was released from the police station. The desk sergeant, though different from the one who had been on duty the night before, was apparently under instructions to make the prisoner aware of the enormity of his crime. He made a big production of returning Charles's bag, his pocket contents, shoelaces and belt. All of the sergeant's slow actions were accompanied by a litany of reproof and when finally allowed to depart, Charles slunk out of the police station like a beaten schoolboy leaving the headmaster's study.

The first thing he did was find a pub and down a couple of large Bell's. To his annoyance, he found some lines of verse repeating in his head.

> I know not whether Laws be right,
> Or whether Laws be wrong;
> All that we know who lie in gaol
> Is that the wall is strong;
> And that each day is like a year,
> A year whose days are long.

Really, after sixteen hours in a police cell, it was a bit much to be quoting *The Ballad of Reading Gaol*!

He stared out of the pub window at the grey November clouds, trying not do it with 'a wistful eye', nor to think of what he was looking at, 'that little tent of blue/Which prisoners call the sky'.

And he thought about the case. Up until then any thinking he'd done about Martin Earnshaw's disappearance had been detached, a prurient general interest shared with the millions who watched *Public Enemies*. Nothing about it touched Charles Paris personally; there had been nothing to awake his own dormant investigative instinct.

Now somehow his attitude had changed. It wasn't the activities of Greg Marchmont the night before; it was the sight of the 'tramp' that had done it. Charles felt certain he had been following Ted Faraday in disguise; and that idea fired his curiosity.

The other stimulus to Charles's interest was Roscoe's overreaction to the idea of his involvement. Surely the superintendent wouldn't have made such a fuss unless he thought there was something about the case Charles Paris was likely to find out.

He moved from the Bell's to a pint of bitter and ordered a steak-and-kidney pudding to erase the memory of his police-station breakfast. Then he rang WET from the pub's payphone.

'Louise Denning, please.'

He was put through to the gallery of the *Public Enemies* studio and the researcher herself answered. 'Yes?'

'Hello. It's Charles Paris.'

'Oh,' she said in a tone of voice that meant 'Why?'

'I thought you might have been trying to contact me.'

'No.'

'It's just that I've been . . . well, a bit tied up, and, er . . .'

'I told you – I haven't been trying to contact you,' she repeated in a tone of voice that meant 'Why should I want to?'

'I just thought I should check in . . .'

'Oh.'

'. . . you know, to see if I might be needed today for the studio or anything.'

'No, you're not.' And with her habitual charm, Louise Denning put the phone down.

Charles Paris went back to his drink and found his steak-and-kidney pie had just been delivered. As he sat down to eat it, he decided he'd stay another night in Brighton.

Charles had no difficulty booking into a cheap hotel, and amused himself until dark with a bottle of Bell's and indistinct children's programmes on the crackling television. Then he walked back through the dark streets of Brighton to Trafalgar Lane.

It was about six when he got there. Once again the light was on in the flat above the second-hand clothes shop. First checking that there wasn't another Kevin Littlejohn lurking in the shadows, Charles moved into the doorway of a boarded-up shop opposite and watched. He thought he discerned occasional flickers of shadowy movement in the flat, but he couldn't be sure.

After about an hour he got bored. Well, that is not strictly true. He got bored after five minutes, but it was only after an hour that he felt so bored he had to do something about the situation or go mad.

He decided to try an old schoolboy trick – ringing the doorbell and running away. The doorway in which he was hiding was too exposed, so he checked out another further along the road before putting his plan into action. He wouldn't be seen there, but should get a good view of anyone who came to the door.

He pressed the broken bell-push, uncertain whether or not it would be working, then scurried off to his hideaway. There he waited.

Just when he had given up hope, decided that either the bell wasn't working or there was no one in the flat, the door was cautiously opened. The hand that opened it appeared to be wearing a rubber glove.

For a moment Charles feared that, seeing no one there, who-ever it was would go straight back inside. But no, a figure in shirt-sleeves stepped out on the pavement and looked in each direction before stepping back inside and closing the door behind him.

The man was out there long enough and there was sufficient light for Charles to recognize Greg Marchmont.

An hour and a half later Charles Paris still maintained his vigil, but with diminished conviction. It was bloody cold, apart from anything else. And what was he hoping to see, for God's sake?

He looked at his watch, registered it was twenty to nine, and suddenly remembered *Public Enemies*.

It was the let-off he'd been waiting for. Convincing himself that he couldn't hope to find out anything about the case without the very latest information, Charles Paris rushed back to his hotel and was snugly settled into his armchair with a large Bell's by the time the opening credits started.

Because of the hotel set's poor reception, Bob Garston looked grittier than ever as he promised 'yet another startling revelation later in the programme – a gruesome new twist in the investigation into the murder of Martin Earnshaw'.

Once again, the audience was teased by trailers through a sequence of more or less irrelevant criminal features until the moment of maximum impact arrived.

Bob Garston back-announced an item about self-switching security sensors and turned gravely to another camera.

'Now the murder of Martin Earnshaw ... Police investigations into the crime are of course continuing and we've had another faxed report from our very own private eye Ted Faraday assuring us he's still on the case. But we also have a startling new development.

'On last week's programme *Public Enemies* brought you exclusive coverage of the ghastly discovery of the dead man's arms ...' He let the pause linger, relishing it. 'This week another, equally gruesome and appalling find has been made. I regret to have to tell you this ...' Oh no you don't, oh no you don't, thought Charles. You're over the moon about it. '. . . but only today a pair of dismembered legs have been discovered.'

Bob Garston left space for the nation's collective gasp before continuing. 'Early tests suggest that these match the arms found last week. Needless to say, today's discovery is yet another indication of the kind of sick mind behind this appalling crime. This particular "Public Enemy" is without scruples or compassion, a cold-blooded monster . . .'

And a brilliant television scheduler, thought Charles.

'And I can assure all of you,' Bob Garston went on, 'that I, and all of the other members of the *Public Enemies* team, will not rest until we have tracked down this merciless killer. Don't worry – with the help of you, the public, we can do it!'

After this crusading climax, he passed over to 'DI Sam Noakes for the details of today's macabre discovery'.

She looked as good as ever, though, after what he'd heard from Greg Marchmont, Charles was even more aware of the hardness in her face.

'At just before eleven o'clock this morning,' the detective inspector announced, 'a passenger from a London train arrived at Brighton station. He went to the car park to retrieve his car, but as he was driving away, noticed a polythene-wrapped package which must have been pushed under the vehicle while it was parked. He looked at the package and, becoming alarmed about its contents, summoned the police. The polythene was opened and inside were discovered the severed legs of a man probably in his fifties.'

Sam Noakes left it there. The dramatic impact, all the *Public Enemies* professionals knew, would be greatest without any comment.

The camera cut back to Bob Garston, now so gritty that he could have got a job as a pithead.

'Needless to say, Martin Earnshaw's wife Chloe is devastated by this latest development. We know, from the letters and phone calls the programme has received for her, how much all of you out there sympathize with her sufferings, and I can assure you that she is very aware of and grateful for . . . your support.'

The presenter had by now turned up his Sincerity Control almost to danger point. 'And I'm sure you know that the best thing you – and we on *Public Enemies* – can do for Chloe Earnshaw . . . is to come up with that vital piece of information that will lead us to her husband's killer.

'So . . . just to see if this jogs anyone's memory – and if it does, remember our phone lines are open twenty-four hours a day – here is a reconstruction – with Chloe Earnshaw pluckily playing herself – of the last time she saw her husband, as he went out . . . "just to have a drink" . . . only a few short weeks ago.'

As the reconstruction began, Charles couldn't help reflecting that his double act with Chloe Earnshaw really had now got top billing.

But that thought was swamped by another shocking realization.

Now he felt certain he knew what had been in the package the 'tramp' had been carrying the night before.

No light showed from the flat when Charles got back to Trafalgar Lane. He pressed long and hard on the bell-push, this time with no thoughts of concealment.

But there was no response. No one came.

He tried the handle. The door was locked, but felt loose and feeble in its crumbling frame. Too excited for caution, Charles Paris threw himself shoulder first at the door. Just like they do in the movies.

There were two shocks. First, how much it hurt his shoulder. And, second, that, in a splintering of rotten wood, the door gave inwards.

He rushed up the dark stairs, certain that the flat was empty.

He should have brought a torch, but was reckless now and, when he opened the door to the front room, switched on the light.

The space was completely empty and smelt of detergent. Every surface gleamed. Some of the paintwork was still sticky and the floorboards damp. The cleaning-up job had been extremely thorough.

He searched through the sitting room, tiny kitchen, lavatory and bathroom, but there was nothing. Every trace of recent occupancy had been erased.

Only on the floorboards of the bathroom was there anything that might constitute a clue. The area was damper than its surrounds, and had clearly been subject to even more vigorous scrubbing.

But two stubborn marks had resisted all the cleaner's efforts. Two spots, each about the size of a new penny piece.

They were rusty, the colour of dried blood.

Chapter Twelve

It was a dilemma. Charles Paris felt certain he had found out something of real significance in the Martin Earnshaw case, but he didn't know what to do about it. His natural instinct would have been to take his findings to the police, but what police? Of those he knew connected with *Public Enemies*, Greg Marchmont quite possibly had some part in the actual crime, and the terms in which Superintendent Roscoe had warned Charles off further investigation ruled him out as a sympathetic ear.

The only officer he felt inclined to inform was Sam Noakes. From what he now knew of the detective inspector's ambition, Charles reckoned she'd welcome new leads to follow up. To have cracked the case apparently single-handed was just the kind of entry she'd like to see on her c.v.

But Charles didn't know where to contact her, and anyway wasn't quite ready to do so yet. He needed to get his own ideas on the case clear first.

These thoughts went through his head as he sat over his hotel breakfast. It was a step up from the police station, but only just. Bacon, egg, shrivelled tomato and soggy fried bread slithered about his plate on a little slick of grease. Nor did the fact that all the other deterrently silent denizens of the tiny dining room were smoking add to Charles's enjoyment.

Also he felt the dull thud of another hangover. He'd needed a few slurps of Bell's to calm him down when he got back the previous night, and they had had a disproportionate effect on his head. It all comes of not drinking the night before, he thought wryly. When you start again, the stuff really does feel powerful. Oh dear, getting back into the old cycle again. Must cut down.

Wouldn't be that hard to have a few days completely off the booze, would it, he tried to convince himself.

With an effort he brought his tired mind to bear on the murder of Martin Earnshaw – in which he felt increasingly certain both Ted Faraday and Greg Marchmont were involved, though at what level he did not know. Marchmont, he was sure, had done the clean-up of the Trafalgar Lane flat. The timing and the fact that the detective sergeant had been in shirt-sleeves and rubber gloves made that certain.

But had he been cleaning up after his own crimes or after those of Ted Faraday? The 'tramp' Charles had seen could not have been Marchmont, who was safely ensconced at the time in the pub where Kevin Littlejohn drank, so it seemed a safe bet that it was Faraday in disguise. Roscoe had certainly pointed up the connection between the private investigator and a flat in Trafalgar Lane.

If the contents of the 'tramp's' package were what Charles strongly suspected, Faraday's involvement became even more chilling. Why would he be carrying the dead man's legs, presumably to their hiding place in the car park, if he had not had a hand in Martin Earnshaw's murder?

If he had, didn't the meticulous cleaning-up operation and the stubborn bloodstains that had survived it suggest that, if not the actual killing, then at least the dismemberment had taken place in the flat?

What the private investigator's motive for murder might have been Charles had no idea. But he remembered Greg Marchmont speaking of Faraday's investigation into a loan-sharking operation and his possibly too close involvement with the criminals concerned. It was Martin Earnshaw's escalating debts to loan sharks that were believed to have led to his murder.

Difficult to get much further without talking to someone. Maybe it would have to be Roscoe or Marchmont after all. Charles decided he would check whether the two policemen were still in Brighton, and rang through to the hotel where they had all stayed.

No, the two gentlemen had checked out the previous day.

Fortunately Charles then asked if any other members of the police were currently staying at the hotel or expected in the near future.

'One of them's booked in for tonight,' the girl replied, with a lack of discretion that suggested she was new to the hotel business. 'That lady policeman . . . you know, the pretty one from the telly.'

'DI Noakes?' said Charles, wondering how Sam would have reacted to her description.

'That's the one. She's arriving after lunch.' A note of doubt came into the girl's voice. 'Ooh, perhaps I shouldn't have told you that.'

'Don't worry about it,' said Charles Paris, as he put the phone down.

There was one small detail of investigation he could undertake on his own before trying to contact Sam Noakes. He consulted the local Yellow Pages. To his surprise, he found no entry under 'Fax', but then he knew that reading Yellow Pages often involved lateral thinking and cross-reference. Indeed, one of his favourite jokes was an entry he'd found in the Yellow Pages: '*Boring*: SEE CIVIL ENGINEERS.'

He found what he wanted under 'Facsimile Bureaux'. 'PRINTSERVE' was there, with an address in Churchill Square. He thought of ringing them, but decided an in-person approach might be more fruitful. So he paid his bill and left the hotel without regret. His lips were still slicked with the taste of that breakfast.

As he walked through Brighton, with the sexy whiff of the sea in his nostrils, Charles Paris tried to decide how to conduct his enquiry at the fax bureau. The direct approach might yield results, but he felt an urge to take on a character for the task. Partly he thought it might get a better response, and partly he was just an old ham.

He went into a tatty junk shop and bought a pair of thick wire-framed glasses. As he put them on, he felt the little lift of excitement taking on a new identity always prompted.

Now who . . . ? Perhaps he should present himself as something to do with the police . . . ? That would at least give a reason for his making the enquiry. It would also give him the guilty *frisson* of breaking the law. Impersonating a policeman he knew to be an offence, but Charles Paris relished some kind of quiet revenge for the dressing-down he'd received from Superintendent Roscoe.

But who exactly should it be? Mentally he reviewed his gallery of policeman performances. They divided naturally into three: those who'd had speeches beginning, 'We have reason to believe . . .'; those who'd said, 'I'm afraid I have some bad news for you, Mrs Blank . . .'; and those who'd shouted, 'Not so fast!'

His favourites perhaps had been seen at a Soho fringe theatre in the early seventies ('Charles Paris's policeman was clearly intended by the author to provide comic relief in this depressing farrago. His was the only performance that didn't make me laugh.' – *Time Out*), and on an extended tour of a sub-Agatha Christie epic called *Murder at the Bishop's Palace*, in which he'd appeared in Act Three to arrest the murderer all the way from Winchester to Wilmslow and attracted from the *Nottingham Evening Post* the ambivalent notice: 'The cast was completed by Charles Paris.'

For the first he had used a vague burr slightly West of Mummerset, and for the second he thought he'd been using Glaswegian until someone he met backstage congratulated him because 'it's so rare to hear a Belfast accent actually done right'.

As he entered PRINTSERVE he still hadn't decided which of these to plump for and in fact, when he came to speak, found himself falling back on a slightly roughened version of his own accent.

'Erm, excuse me,' he said to the pert-looking girl busy at the photocopier.

She replied with a preoccupied 'Mm?'

Charles went straight into law-breaking mode. 'I'm a police officer.'

'Oh yes?' She turned to face him. 'Have you got any identification?'

Damn. This girl had watched too much television. He reached into his jacket for his wallet, trying desperately to remember what he'd got in it that might vaguely look like an identity card. She wasn't going to be fooled by Visa or Access, was she? Or by the video membership he'd once taken out and then never got round to buying a VCR?

But just as he was contemplating an ignominious retreat from the shop, his hand closed round a piece of paper, which he remembered was a letter confirming his filming schedule from the *Public Enemies* office at WET. That would have to do.

'As you'll see from this . . .' He flashed the letterhead at the girl '. . . I am currently seconded to the *Public Enemies* programme . . .'

'Ooh yes!' Television worked its customary magic on yet another member of the British public. 'I watched that last night. It's horrible, isn't it? I mean particularly with the Martin Earnshaw murder having taken place right here in Brighton. That poor wife of his . . . And what kind of sick mind would cut a body up like that? It's almost as if he's actually staging the discovery of the bits in time for the programmes, isn't it?'

This echoed a suspicion which had formed more than once in Charles's mind, but he made no comment, simply pressed on with his enquiry. 'It's about the *Public Enemies* programme that I'm calling, in fact. As you know, we've been asking members of the public to send in information and—'

''Ere,' said the girl. 'You look a bit like him.'

'A bit like who?'

'Martin Earnshaw. The bloke who was murdered.'

'Do I? Really?' Charles Paris screwed up his eyes behind the glasses to look as unmartinearnshawlike as possible. 'Well, nobody's ever said that to me before. Perhaps it's just because the case is on your mind that you're seeing likenesses that aren't there.'

'Perhaps ...' the girl reluctantly agreed.

'Now as I say, in the *Public Enemies* office we get information from all over the country and a lot of it comes by fax. Some of these faxes we like to check up on, just to see whether they're authentic or not, and there was one sent from this office earlier in the week...'

'Sent to *Public Enemies?*'

'Yes.'

'Ooh. Which day was it?'

Charles did a quick calculation of when he'd been in the *Public Enemies* office. 'Tuesday. About quarter past eleven.'

'I'll look at the journal,' said the girl.

She quickly found the details on the print-out. 'This is a London number. That the right one?'

Charles checked it against the letterhead. 'Yes.'

'All right then. I can confirm that it was sent from here. Is that all you wanted to know?'

'I wonder if by any chance you can remember who it was who sent it ... ?'

The girl racked her brains and, with a bit of prompting, managed to come up with a rough description.

Though the fax purportedly came from him, her description certainly didn't fit Ted Faraday.

Indeed, the only person involved in the case it could have fitted was Greg Marchmont.

*

125

'I know you, don't I?' said Sam Noakes, as she opened the door of her hotel room.

'Well, I'm Martin Earnshaw.' Her eyes narrowed, suspicious for a moment that she was up against a crank. 'That is to say, my name is Charles Paris. I'm the actor who's playing Martin Earnshaw in the reconstructions.'

'Oh, right, of course. Sorry, should have recognized you straight away. Won't you sit down?'

She gestured to the chair in front of the dressing table, and sat herself on the side of the double bed. It was just an ordinary room, more or less identical to the one Charles had had in the same hotel. Sam Noakes had suggested he should join her there to avoid the security risks of the public rooms, and he was sure that was part of her reason. But he also detected in it a kind of feminist bravado, inviting a strange man up to her room to show how unaffected she was by the cautions other women might have felt. There was even perhaps an element of challenge, to test out the reception he'd get if he did try anything on.

Trying anything on, however, was the last thought on Charles Paris's mind. Though Sam Noakes carried a permanent aura of sexuality and looked good in jeans and loose-fitting jumper, he would have sooner tangled with a boa constrictor. Even before Greg Marchmont had told him about her character, Charles had identified Sam Noakes as dangerous territory. Anyway, he wasn't in the habit of making advances in hotel rooms to women he didn't know. Well, certainly not when he was sober.

'So . . . what is it, Mr Paris? You said when you phoned it was something to do with the Earnshaw case.'

'Yes. It is.'

'Have you been making your own enquiries into it? We've already got one private investigator on the strength. Does every aspiring gumshoe in the country now feel entitled to have a go?'

'If they do, then programmes like *Public Enemies* are as much to blame as anything else.'

She nodded, conceding the truth of this. 'Yes, well, I guess we are encouraging people to be observant, take note of any information that might be useful. What have you got for us, Mr Paris – a clue?'

'Maybe. A lead, anyway. Certainly something that might be worthy of further investigation.'

'Tell me about it.'

And he told her. Sam Noakes listened impassively, her pale blue eyes steady, reacting neither to his mentions of Greg Marchmont nor Ted Faraday. At the end she shook her red hair and asked, 'Why do you think there's any connection between the flat and Faraday?'

'Superintendent Roscoe mentioned Trafalgar Lane when we were talking about Faraday going undercover in Brighton. What he said to Sergeant Marchmont certainly implied that it was from there that Faraday was conducting his investigations.'

'Except what you said implied that his involvement with Martin Earnshaw was rather more sinister than just investigation.'

'Well . . .'

'Accusing someone of murder is a pretty serious allegation, Mr Paris . . .'

'I know.'

'. . . and not one that should be bandied about lightly.'

'No.'

'And I'm not quite sure what it is you're accusing Greg of, but I'd be pretty careful about that too, if I were you.'

'Yes,' Charles agreed humbly.

'It is possible, you see, that you have by chance stumbled on part of the police investigation and completely misconstrued what's been going on.'

'I suppose that is possible, yes.'

'You bet your life it is. Mr Paris, I'm very grateful to you for sharing your opinions with me, and I will be even more grateful if you give me your solemn word you will keep quiet about them to anyone else. This investigation is reaching a very critical stage, and the last thing we need at this point is to have the whole thing screwed up by an amateur.'

She didn't raise her voice or put particular emphasis on the final word, but it still stung. It stung all the more because of its aptness. Charles felt totally excluded. The police investigation was proceeding and he was on the outside, without access to any of their skills or information.

But he felt he had to say something in his own defence. 'Look, I know it was Greg Marchmont who cleaned the flat up; and I'm pretty convinced it was Ted Faraday dressed up as the tramp; so the Trafalgar Lane flat has got to have some connection with the case.'

'I'm not denying it has, but isn't it likely that Greg was cleaning the place up because he had been given orders to do so by his superiors? As to the idea that Ted would use as crass a disguise as the one you describe, that alone – apart from all the other wild allegations you've made about him – means that you're certainly one hundred per cent wrong there. You have absolutely no basis for saying that the man you followed *was* Faraday, do you, Mr Paris?'

Charles was forced to admit that he hadn't.

Sam Noakes smiled, evidently taking pity on him. 'Look,' she said, as if soothing a fractious child, '*Public Enemies* is an exciting programme. It's meant to be an exciting programme, and inevitably members of the public get caught up in that excitement. For someone like you, actually involved in the making of the programme, the temptation to get carried away by the whole thing is all the stronger. But just remember – that doesn't justify making allegations against a hard-working member of the police force, based on nothing more than unsubstantiated guesswork.

OK? Television is a glamorous medium, Mr Paris, and some people just can't resist the pull of that glamour.'

Speak for yourself, thought Charles Paris savagely.

If there was one thing he couldn't stand, it was being patronized.

Chapter Thirteen

'I hope the murderer realizes just how much hangs on what he's doing,' said Bob Garston grimly. 'We held steady on last week's overnights, but we didn't get the kind of build in the figures I'd been hoping for.'

'Well, there was the first showing of yet another new Michael Caine movie on Sky,' Roger Parkes offered by way of explanation.

'Come on, bloody satellite shouldn't dent our figures.'

'Beginning to. More serious, though, the BBC had started their umpteenth rerun of *Dad's Army* right opposite us after the News. A lot of people probably switched over for that.'

'Why? There can't be a single person in the country who hasn't seen those seventeen times already. *Public Enemies* is giving them something unprecedented in British television, something of today, reflecting all the violence and ghastliness of modern society. I really can't believe that anyone would prefer the anodyne nostalgic claptrap of *Dad's Army* to what we're offering.'

Roger Parkes shrugged. 'The figures speak for themselves. There are a good few millions out there for whom the reason they have a telly is to watch anodyne nostalgic claptrap.'

'But *Public Enemies* is holding up a mirror to the real world!'

'Plenty of people would do anything to avoid the real world. You know there's always got to be tacky entertainment fluff as well as serious journalism on the box. It's not as if you didn't spend all those years doing *If the Cap Fits*!'

Bob Garston seethed visibly. '*If the Cap Fits*! was not "tacky entertainment fluff". It was the best game show of its kind. I make sure that every show I do is the best of its kind.' His expression found new extremes of grittiness. 'But *Public Enemies* is something even more special. In this show I'm going back to my no-nonsense hard-bitten journalistic roots, bloody well working at the coalface of real life.'

'Yes,' Roger Parkes agreed automatically. He'd heard all this a good few times before.

So had Charles Paris. It was absolutely typical of television people, he thought, that the presenter and producer should continue their conversation as if there was no one else in the room. He'd been summoned to a briefing meeting on the Monday morning and already spent an hour sitting in the *Public Enemies* office without anyone taking any notice of him. There seemed no prospect of his being briefed about anything.

Louise Denning swanned imperiously into the room, brandishing some stapled sheets of paper. 'Got the first audience breakdown on last week's show.'

Bob Garston seized the report eagerly and pored over it.

'What's the general message?' asked Roger Parkes.

Louise Denning screwed up her face. 'A lot of people switched over in the middle of the programme. Round twelve and a half minutes in.'

Bob Garston, despite his furious concentration on the report, had heard this. 'See, Roger. I told you that item on how to make an insurance claim after a burglary was a boring load of shit.'

'It's something we get a lot of enquiries about,' the executive producer replied patiently. It was not the first time they had had this argument.

'Yes, well, we should write back to them with the information, not put it on the bloody screen! "Insurance" is one of those instant switch-off words on television. Like "Northern Ireland" or "European Community" or "Bosnia". I'm going to put a total ban on it. No more mentions of bloody "insurance" on

Public Enemies – ever!' Bob Garston buried himself back in the research.

Roger Parkes raised a wearily interrogative eyebrow to Louise Denning. 'And overall impressions . . . ?'

'General view was the punters enjoyed it, but found it a bit the same as last week's programme. You know, discovery of the arms at the end of one, discovery of the legs at the end of the other. General feeling they'd like the contents varied a bit.'

Roger Parkes grimaced ruefully. 'Well, we're really in the hands of the murderer there, aren't we? I mean, there's no question about the fact that he's aware of the programme. He's an exhibitionist and he gets a charge from the publicity, showing how clever he is and all that. So maybe he's also aware of the need to keep building the excitement – and the figures.'

Bob Garston pushed the research report aside with a disgruntled gesture. 'Yes. If only we could contact him and tell him the kind of thing we need . . .'

'What do you reckon we do need then?' asked the executive producer.

'Some kind of twist on the case, something new . . .' The presenter tapped his teeth impatiently.

'Well, what're we hoping for this week? Presumably the discovery of the torso . . . ? He's never going to go straight to the head, is he?'

'No, no, that'd be like naming an awards winner before you name the nominees – our murderer's got more sense of theatre than that.'

'You don't think,' Roger Parkes suggested ominously, 'he'll have kept the torso and the head together, do you?'

'No, no, of course he won't. He's not a bloody amateur. Anyone who knows the first thing about dismembering is going to take the head off, aren't they? No, we definitely need the torso this week, but we need a bit of an angle on it.'

'Like . . .'

'Well, like the torso being found in an unusual place ... Or being found mutilated in some horrible way ... that'd do. Needs something *sexy* about it ...'

'Hm ...' Roger Parkes shook his head thoughtfully. 'Of course we do have a potential problem, the way he's feeding us the bits, don't we?'

'What do you mean?'

'Well, if, as we're assuming, we've only got the torso and the head to go ... and we get those over the next two weeks, it leaves us with a big hole for Programme Six, doesn't it?'

'I'd thought of that, yes. About the only thing that's really going to pay the series off is if we can actually announce the identity of the murderer in the last programme.'

'Yes, that'd be good,' Roger Parkes agreed. 'Real Hercule Poirot stuff. Invite all of the viewers into the library ... A twirl of the moustaches and ... "You may wonder why I've asked you all here ..."'

Bob Garston was caught up by the idea. 'Like it. The budget'd run to a library set, wouldn't it ... ?'

'If we don't get carried away over the next couple of weeks, yes.'

'Hm ...' A new thought struck Garston. 'You don't think that'd look like trivializing the subject, do you?'

'Oh, *no.*'

'Damn, it's frustrating, isn't it? If only we could contact the murderer and tell him what the programme needs ... that'd make things so much simpler, wouldn't it?'

Am I really hearing this, Charles Paris asked himself.

He sat ignored in the *Public Enemies* office until a quarter to one, when he thought sod this, I'm going to get some lunch. He announced his intention to anyone who might be interested, but nobody appeared to be.

Lunch was of course preceded by a visit to the WET bar.

133

Charles wasn't particularly hungover that day, so he went straight on to the beer. He sat down with the welcome pint at a table commanding a view over rooftops towards Regent's Park, and thought about the conversation he had just heard.

What it did bring home to him once again was how high the stakes were in television. For Bob Garston and Roger Parkes *Public Enemies'* audience share was the greatest priority – indeed their only priority. So far as they were concerned, Martin Earnshaw's murder – and his murderer – existed solely to serve that priority. The fact that a human life had been lost was an irrelevant detail.

Charles wondered how far Garston and Parkes would actually go to make their programme successful. The idea that one or both of them was orchestrating the gradual piecing together of the corpse was incongruous, but not totally incongruous.

There remained no doubt that the murderer was aware of his contribution to *Public Enemies*, and indeed was playing up to the demands of the programme. It would be too much of a coincidence for the timing to be accidental. The murderer was someone who understood television, and knew the impact the reports of his actions had.

So Garston and Parkes could not be ruled out. What would a mere murder signify in their cold-blooded pursuit of ratings? Possibly even Sam Noakes came into the frame too. The unravelling of the murder investigation was certainly doing no harm to her public profile. And if she was as ruthlessly ambitious as Greg Marchmont had maintained, was it ridiculous to think of her controlling events, or of having killed Martin Earnshaw herself?

Charles's instinctive answer to this question was no, but, moving on from that thought, he wondered whether Greg Marchmont might have committed the crime on her behalf. The sergeant was clearly still besotted. He'd said he'd do anything for her. Could that anything go as far as committing a murder, either at her instigation, or with a view to regaining her favour? Again it seemed incongruous, but Greg Marchmont's actions did seem suspicious. He had definitely done the cleaning-up job on the Trafalgar Lane flat, and had also sent the fax purporting to have come from Ted Faraday.

The private investigator was someone else whose actions required further investigation. If Faraday had been the 'tramp' Charles followed, then they required very close investigation. But Ted Faraday remained a shadowy figure, only encountered that once in the hospitality suite and since then vanished undercover.

Charles Paris felt confused and out of touch. It wasn't even his investigation, the police presumably had everything in hand, but he was frustrated by the tantalizing anomalies and pointers that he had accumulated.

He looked down at his empty glass. Another pint might help. Wouldn't do any harm, anyway.

While he was waiting at the counter behind a drama producer who'd just finished a play and had a shipping order of drinks for his cast and crew, Charles saw a familiar figure come into the bar and look round for someone. It was Sam Noakes, smartly dressed in beige jacket and trousers.

He caught her eye. She recognized him immediately this time. 'Can I get you a drink?' he offered.

'I'm meeting someone, actually.'

'Quick one while you're waiting?'

The barman had just become free. 'OK,' said Sam. 'Dry white wine, please.'

Charles got the drinks and led her across to his table.

'I'll have to leave you when he arrives, Mr Paris.'

'Sure, sure. No problem. Cheers.' They raised their glasses and looked out towards the treetops of Regent's Park. 'So, any dramatic breakthroughs on the case, DI?' he asked in his best American police series voice.

135

She smiled. He noticed that she had made herself up with some care that morning. 'You know, even if there were, I wouldn't be able to tell you, Mr Paris.'

'Oh, come on,' he wheedled, keeping the tone light. 'I was the one who put you on to the flat in Brighton – don't I at least get told where that fits into the case?'

Her face darkened. 'Very well. You get told that it has nothing at all to do with the case.'

'But—'

'Mr Paris, the flat has been examined and ruled out as having no relevance to our enquiries.'

'When you say "examined", do you mean "forensically examined"? I'm sure those were bloodstains on the—'

'The flat was given all necessary examination. Forensic resources are expensive and only deployed when there is good reason for them to be deployed.' A bitterness came into her tone. 'I would have liked more forensic investigation used in this case – though not into that flat, as it happens . . .'

'Into the body parts that have been found?'

She nodded. 'Oh, all the basic stuff's been done – confirming the arms and legs belonged to the same person, that kind of thing, but I think more detailed examination could be conducted at this stage.' She shrugged. 'Others don't share my opinion, however. There is a view that more useful conclusions can be drawn when all of the body parts have been recovered. I don't happen to share that view, but—' She shrugged again '—I'm not in charge of the case.'

'And Superintendent Roscoe is?'

'He's in charge of certain aspects of the case.' She couldn't keep the contempt out of her voice. 'At least in name.'

'And he's seeing that it's being conducted in a good, old-fashioned, traditional way?'

Sam Noakes smiled at Charles, and once again he could feel

her sexual magnetism. 'You're not going to draw me into criticism of a fellow officer, Mr Paris.'

'Oh . . . spoilsport.' This prompted a girlish grin, thawing the atmosphere sufficiently for him to probe a little further. 'So did you actually find out what Greg Marchmont was doing in that flat?'

The temperature immediately dropped again. 'Sergeant Marchmont has been taken off the case. He's on sick leave at the moment.'

'Oh. But what do you think he was doing at—?'

'Mr Paris, I thought I'd made clear in Brighton what my views are about amateurs getting involved in police investigations.'

'Yes, but—'

She looked across the bar and rose to her feet. 'You must excuse me. Thank you for the drink.'

His eyes followed her across the room. To his surprise the person she greeted with a little peck on the cheek was Bob Garston. Together they walked through to the executive dining room.

Of course there were a hundred and one programme-related reasons for the two of them to be having lunch together, but something about their body language suggested a more personal motivation.

And why not? Bob Garston was always so preoccupied with work that Charles had never speculated about his sex life. Presumably he had one, though, and no doubt he brought to it the same kind of single-mindedness he did to everything else.

And for Sam Noakes he probably represented a valuable prize. In spite of her apparent poise, she shared the fascination of her colleagues with show business. To be seen around with Bob Garston wouldn't do her image in the force any harm at all.

Also, someone controlling the power of Bob's Your Uncle

Productions might be very useful to the burgeoning media career of Detective Inspector Sam Noakes.

Charles took advantage of the WET subsidized canteen to have roast pork and two veg, followed by treacle roll and custard. With a couple of glasses of red wine. Very civilized.

Then he went back to the *Public Enemies* suite, wondering without much optimism whether his briefing meeting would ever happen.

The office was unlocked and empty, a most unusual state of affairs. The *Public Enemies* team made an enormous production out of their security procedures, constantly punching codes into locks and sliding cards with magnetic strips into slots. Possibly now, midway into the series, everyone was getting lax in their vigilance. Or maybe Bob Garston, distracted by the thought of his lunch date, had forgotten to give his customary exhortations about the importance of security.

Still, it was not an opportunity Charles Paris was going to pass up. He moved quickly across to Louise Denning's desk and started flicking through the card index she kept there. He went straight to 'Marchmont', against whose name the words 'Roscoe's Gofer' had been written, and made a note of the address and phone number.

He flicked on to 'Noakes', and took down her home and office numbers. Against her name had been written the single word 'Star'.

Since he was so close alphabetically, he turned up his own card. Beside his name were scrawled the words 'Corpse Looka-like'. Hm, thought Charles Paris, always nice for an actor to have his artistry appreciated.

He heard a movement in the outside office, closed the index box and sat down. One of the secretaries entered, looking rather guilty, aware that she shouldn't have left the office unattended.

The rest of the production team came back from lunch over

the next half-hour, and all studiously ignored Charles Paris. Eventually, round four, Louise Denning announced to the room at large that they'd decided they weren't going to do any more reconstruction on the Martin Earnshaw case that week.

'Does that mean I won't be needed?' asked Charles.

The researcher looked at him as if he'd just crawled out from underneath something. 'Well, of course it does.'

'I was told to come here for a briefing meeting, you see.'

'Well, if there isn't going to be any reconstruction, I'd hardly have thought there was going to be any briefing for it, would you?' she asked, heavily sarcastic.

'No. It's just that I've been sitting here for the last two hours, you haven't taken any calls about the reconstruction during that time, so presumably you've known for at least two hours that I wouldn't be needed?'

Louise Denning acknowledged with a shrug that this was indeed the case.

Charles was about to launch into a tirade about common courtesy, but then thought, why bother? She's probably never heard of the word.

The researcher ungraciously gave him permission to leave. 'But don't go away or anything. The situation could change. We might need to contact you.'

As he went out of the *Public Enemies* office, it occurred to him that Bob Garston hadn't come back from lunch yet.

There was no reply from Greg Marchmont's number when Charles tried it from the Hereford Road payphone. He looked at the address he'd scribbled down. Only Ladbroke Groveish . . .

Why not? Not as if he had a lot else to do.

Greg Marchmont had a basement flat in a rather dingy building. Presumably when married with children he'd owned a house somewhere. This was what he had been reduced to by his infatuation with Sam Noakes.

An arrow painted on the wall identified '57B' and pointed down crumbling concrete steps. Charles went down and pressed the discoloured plastic bell-push. It elicited no response. But then he couldn't hear any ringing, so maybe it wasn't working.

He banged on the door. Nothing. And again. Still nothing.

He moved from the door to the grubby, barred window. Sunbleached curtains had been drawn across, but did not quite meet. Charles peered through the uneven slit, trying to make out the room's murky interior.

It doubled as bedroom and sitting room. A tangle of sheets and tartan blanket lay on the open sofabed. Clothes, newspapers, glasses and coffee cups littered most surfaces. An old record player perched on a brassbound pine chest. A battered kettle and stained pressure cooker sat on gas rings.

Charles had to admit, with some shame, that it did all look horribly like home.

But there was no sign of anyone in there. He tapped on the window.

Nothing stirred.

DS Greg Marchmont might be on sick leave, but he certainly wasn't at home in bed.

Chapter Fourteen

That Thursday's *Public Enemies* began differently from the previous ones. Bob Garston and Roger Parkes had taken to heart the public's message about predictability, and completely changed the format of the programme.

Throughout the day trailers had done their teasing work, suggesting the imminence of another sensational first for television. But the viewing audience is canny. In a world where every programme is hyped way beyond its possible value, they have learned to take the claims of trailers with a healthy pinch of scepticism.

When that week's *Public Enemies* started, though, they were left in no doubt they were in for something different. The continuity announcer gave the kind of lead-in that all such programmes covet. 'And now it's time for this week's *Public Enemies* which, because of the nature of the subject matter, contains some sequences which certain viewers may find disturbing.'

Faint hearts immediately switched over to the BBC News and *Dad's Army*. The majority who remained tuned to ITV, pleasantly titillated by the introductory announcement, were then shocked by the absence of the familiar *Public Enemies* signature tune and credits. Instead, they saw a close-up of a knotted string against brown paper.

The image shifted slightly as if in motion and, as the camera drew back, the detail was revealed to be part of a paper-wrapped rectangular parcel about four foot high. It was being pushed on a trolley by a uniformed security guard into what Charles Paris – watching through the customary blizzard at Hereford Road – recognized as the *Public Enemies* office.

During the camera's pull-back, a sonorous voice-over from Bob Garston began. 'On tonight's *Public Enemies* you can witness live a bizarre and horrible manifestation of the criminal mind in action. Yesterday afternoon, *this* package was delivered by a commercial courier company to WET House. Its label [THE CAMERA LINGERED ON THE LABEL] was addressed to this programme, so it was brought up to our office.

[BOB GARSTON CAME INTO SHOT, AS THE SECURITY MAN STOPPED HIS TROLLEY AND MOVED THE PACKAGE TO THE HORIZONTAL.]

'I myself removed the outer packing from the parcel. [BOB GARSTON WAS SEEN TO CUT THE STRING AND REMOVE SOME OF THE BROWN PAPER]. And I immediately saw *this* notice stuck on the next layer of wrapping.

[THE CAMERA HOMED IN ON A PRINTED NOTICE ON RED PAPER, STUCK ON TO THE NEXT LAYER OF WHITE PAPER WRAPPING THE RECTANGLE. THE NOTICE READ:

WHY NOT HAVE THE CAMERA RUNNING WHEN YOU OPEN THIS LITTLE BOX OF GOODIES? YOU MIGHT FIND IT INTERESTING.

PUBLIC ENEMY NO. 1]

'Because I thought it might serve the public interest by helping to solve a crime, I decided we would follow the suggestion of whoever it was who had dubbed himself "Public Enemy No. 1", and we filmed the opening of the parcel – with sensational results which you will see throughout the rest of the programme. I should warn viewers of a nervous disposition that they may find some of what follows . . . upsetting.

'This sequence you are now watching is a reconstruction. Until we saw the message we obviously had not thought of having our cameras ready. But everything else you will see throughout the programme was filmed live – exactly as it happened.'

The ponderous voice-over stopped, the camera homed in on the printed notice, and that image mixed to the usual *Public Enemies* opening credits. Throughout the country millions of viewers thought, if they didn't actually say out loud, 'That package looks just about the right size to hold a human torso.'

After the credits, Bob Garston gave another little teaser about the opening of the package, before introducing an innocuous fill-in item on the methods used by counterfeiters and ways of spotting counterfeit banknotes. It was pretty dull, but at least it didn't mention the word 'insurance'.

Then, momentously, the presenter announced that they would show the next stage in the opening of the mystery package.

It had been moved from the office and the trolley was no longer in evidence. The white-wrapped oblong stood like a gravestone in a studio set of white tiles and chromium tubes, which suggested the image of a forensic pathology lab. Uniformed police, including Sam Noakes, stood by, as well as medical-looking white-coated figures. Everyone had rubber gloves on.

Bob Garston, dressed in white coat and rubber gloves, stepped forward and talked himself through his actions in the way beloved of regional news reporters.

'Well, I'll just tear off this sellotape here and pull off this corner of the paper. I'm afraid I'm going to have to tear it a bit. Ah, it looks like there's something wooden underneath. Yes, I'll just move a bit more of the paper and . . . ah, here we go. Strip the rest off and . . . There it is.'

With the remains of the paper jumbled on the floor like clothes someone had just stepped out of, what stood revealed was a wooden chest about four feet by two feet by two feet.

In silence the camera homed in on this. Then the filmed

insert ended and they cut back to Bob Garston live on the regular *Public Enemies* set.

'In a few minutes you'll see the next stage of our opening that package, but first an update on some of the art works that have been recovered following the raid on Birmingham's Merton Frinsley Gallery in July.'

The great British public sat through another more or less tedious item. Only a few hands strayed to remote controls, opting for the familiar warm bath of *Dad's Army*.

Then, after the agony had been extended by a further link from Bob Garston, the programme cut back to the wooden chest in the forensic pathology lab. Garston, in his white coat, watched silently as two uniformed police officers (wearing rubber gloves of course) ceremoniously moved the chest over to the horizontal. The camera moved in on the brass latch that held it closed.

Bob Garston's voice was heard again. 'Don't know whether this is going to be locked or not. We do have a police expert with a picklock on hand if that should prove necessary, but let's see . . .'

His rubber-gloved hands came into shot. 'It may just be on the latch, so I'll try that first.' The hands fumbled with the latch, pressing in a button and trying to raise the chest's lid. These actions took longer than was strictly necessary, as Bob Garston milked the drama of the situation.

'No, I don't think it's . . . Oh, just a minute, maybe it's . . . No. One more try and . . . yes, I think it is going to open.'

Very slowly he lifted the lid. The camera veered away a little and moved round to peer over his shoulder, almost exactly reproducing the presenter's point of view as he looked downwards.

Inside the chest was revealed a bulky object, wrapped in a tartan rug.

The viewers only had a moment's sight of this, an almost subliminal flash, before they were whisked back to live action in the studio.

Bob Garston, promising 'more of that footage later in the programme', then introduced an achingly boring feature about new anti-theft devices for cars. But *Dad's Army* didn't gain any more viewers. The audience for *Public Enemies* was far too caught up in the ghoulish scenario that was unfolding before them.

The next insert of film was very short. Bob Garston's rubber-gloved hands were seen beginning to unwrap the tartan blanket in the chest, then the camera cut sharply to his face. Sudden shock registered there, as he gasped, 'Quick, police surgeon!'

The programme's final prerecorded feature – about a group of pensioner vigilantes who had banded together to fight crime on a Newcastle housing estate – seemed to last for ever. But finally Bob Garston cued back to the set with the chest.

It was totally transformed now. Policemen bustled in every direction. There were photographers and men picking at things with tweezers. There was lots of plastic sheeting all over the place. It looked like a classic scene of the crime.

The edges of the tartan blanket spilled out of the chest, so that its contents must have been exposed.

But the camera did not show what was inside. Not quite. It showed everything else, darting around, catching odd angles of the chest, approaching as if to reveal more, then sliding off when it drew close. It was the camerawork of the strip-tease, the technique that was used in all those nude movies of the early sixties which kept avoiding the hairy bits.

And in the middle of all this chaos stood Bob Garston. He was very pale (whether naturally or through the ministrations of the make-up department was hard to know) and he had on the grittiest expression even he had ever attained.

'Ladies and gentlemen,' he announced grimly, 'I can now inform you that the contents of that chest are . . .' He held the pause with the skill of a professional torturer '. . . a human torso.' And the programme ended.

*

145

Half the country shuddered gleefully in communal shock.

But no one was more shocked than Charles Paris. He recognized the tartan blanket and the brassbound chest. He had last seen them in Greg Marchmont's flat.

Chapter Fifteen

It was only a twenty-minute walk, but Charles picked up a cab in Westbourne Grove and gave the driver Greg Marchmont's address. He hadn't worked out what he was going to do when he arrived, just knew he had to get there as quickly as possible.

As he hurried down the stairs he could see a light on through the basement curtains. His excitement took him beyond fear. Some kind of confrontation was now inevitable. He raised his hand to bang on the door.

But then he noticed it was slightly ajar. Charles pushed and the door gave silently inwards.

He stepped into the tiny hall, off which two doors gave, one on to the bedsitting room, the other presumably to a bathroom. The sitting-room door was also ajar.

'Hello?' said Charles softly. 'Is there anyone there? Greg?'

No voice answered him; nor was there any sound of movement. He pushed the door open and sidled into the sitting room.

The first thing he noticed was that the brassbound pine chest was missing. Nor was there any sign of the tartan rug in the disarray of sheets on the sofabed.

Otherwise the room looked even more of a mess than it had the previous day. Drawers of a desk hung open and papers were scattered all over the floor.

Charles bent down to look at these and found all the symptoms of a life fallen apart. There were stern letters from bank managers, statements showing overdrafts galloping out of control, final demands for telephone and gas bills. On Metropolitan Police headed notepaper was a vigorous denunciation from a chief superintendent, assuring Detective Sergeant Marchmont that if there was any repetition of the incident when he was drunk on duty, his career in the force would be at an end.

There was a cold note about late maintenance payments, signed 'Yours, Maureen'.

And a memento of the cause of the trouble. A faded card with a picture of a satisfied ginger cat on the front. Inside were the words: 'Thanks for last night. It was wonderful. Love, Sam.'

Charles moved across to the desk and looked through its remaining contents. There were more, similar letters, more bank statements, a stiff communication from the building society about mortgage arrears.

And down at the bottom, as if they had been hidden away, two documents which brought a dry nausea to the back of Charles's throat.

On one were typed the following words:

'IF YOU'RE LOOKING FOR MARTIN EARNSHAW, YOU COULD DO WORSE THAN OPEN A COUPLE OF COFFINS IN COLMER.'

On the other the message read:

'IF YOU WANT A BIT MORE OF M. E., YOU MIGHT FIND SOME-THING PARKED AT BRIGHTON STATION.'

Charles inspected the sheets closely. Plain white photocopying paper. And on the back of each a little circular red stamp, indicating that the sheets had been faxed.

It looked as if Charles Paris had found Martin Earnshaw's murderer.

He scanned the sad, anonymous room – its open wardrobe with jumbled clothes spilling out, its gas rings with kettle and pressure cooker, its silent telephone, its air of seedy despair. And once again he felt how close he himself had come to this.

He moved dejectedly back to the hall, uncertain what to do next. Obviously the police must be contacted. But Charles Paris was disinclined to involve himself in the inevitable fuss which would follow. He was suddenly terribly tired, unable to face a long night of explanations and statements. No, an anonymous

999 call was the answer. Put on a voice, mention the Martin Earnshaw case, give Greg Marchmont's address and let the police procedures take their course.

He decided he might as well take a look in the bathroom. Not that he expected to find out anything else. There wasn't really anything else *to* find out.

He turned the handle, opened the door, and looked inside.

Greg Marchmont was slumped on the closed lavatory seat in a parody of drunken collapse. Charles couldn't see the wound, which must have been on the far side of the policeman's head, but blood was spattered over the tiles and cistern and had drenched the right shoulder of his grey pullover.

His right hand dangled, almost apelike, a few inches above the cracked lino. On the floor beneath it lay a black automatic pistol.

Detective Sergeant Greg Marchmont was undoubtedly dead.

Chapter Sixteen

Charles Paris felt numb, almost detached. His mind wasn't working properly. Ideas floated there loosely, unable or perhaps unwilling to make connections.

He forced himself to go closer to the body. He registered that the spattered blood was still bright red and shiny. It had only just stopped flowing, and had not yet begun to dry and turn brown.

With an even greater effort he leant forward to touch the flesh of Greg Marchmont's hand. It was warm. The sergeant had not been long dead.

Then he noticed on the floor a sheet torn from a notebook. On it were scrawled the words:

'I'M SORRY. I THOUGHT I COULD COPE WITH EVERYTHING, BUT WHEN IT CAME DOWN TO IT, I JUST COULDN'T STAND THE PRESSURE'

There was no means of knowing whether the lack of full stop after the last word was just carelessness or whether the message was incomplete. The dutiful use of punctuation in the rest of the message might point to the second conclusion.

Charles Paris backed away. Ring the police. Dial 999 and get the message across. That was the only coherent thought crystallizing in his mind.

He could make the call from where he was. Use Marchmont's phone and then get the hell out of the place. He tried to remember how much Bell's he'd got back at Hereford Road. He was going to need a lot to anaesthetize him that night.

Charles Paris looked at his watch, wondering if he might still find an off-licence open. Twenty-seven minutes past ten. The transmission of *Public Enemies* had finished less than half an hour before. It felt so long ago it could have happened in a previous incarnation.

He moved automatically out of the bathroom, averting his eyes from the corpse, through the hall and back into the sitting room.

He approached the telephone, then hesitated. Was it sensible to make the call from there or might that link him to the place?

Fingerprints. God, his fingerprints were already on the door handles, possibly on the drawers and the papers he had picked up.

A dull panic made its slow progress through him. He was still too traumatized to feel anything stronger.

And with the panic came a new thought, a thought that started as a tiny inkling but quickly grew to a hideous certainty. Maybe Marchmont's message had been unfinished. Maybe it was missing the word 'COOKER'.

Zombie-like, almost in slow motion, as in one of those dreams where you run hopelessly through sand, Charles Paris moved towards the gas rings. He took a handkerchief out of his pocket and wrapped it loosely round the handles of the pressure cooker. Feeling their outlines through the cloth, he eased them apart. He closed his hand round the lid handle and lifted it up.

His intuition was confirmed. In the dry interior of the pressure cooker was a human head.

Mercifully, the eyes were closed, but the shock that ripped through Charles was still intense.

It wasn't the shock, though, of seeing the face of the man he was employed to resemble.

Though discoloured and a little battered, the features were easily recognizable.

The head belonged to Ted Faraday.

Chapter Seventeen

Charles Paris tried to piece it together the following morning on the train down to Brighton. His head felt as if it had been scrubbed by an over-diligent housewife with a pot-scourer. There hadn't been a great deal of Bell's back at Hereford Road, but enough. To his shame he'd bought another half at the Victoria Station off-licence that morning and already made inroads into it. The remaining contents sloshed around noisily in the bottle in his sports jacket pocket.

But, Charles told himself, it wasn't the booze that had made him feel so shitty; it was the fact that he'd hardly slept. Every time he closed his eyes, the screen of his mind had filled with that head in the pressure cooker. On the few occasions when he did doze off, he was quickly woken by a dream of the head in even less wholesome circumstances, steaming away with a selection of vegetables. Through the night he had felt – and still felt – as tight as a coiled spring.

After consideration, he hadn't rung the police. He reckoned they would make the discovery for themselves soon enough. Instead, he'd attempted a few futile gestures with a handkerchief to wipe the surfaces where fingerprints might incriminate him, and left Greg Marchmont's flat, slipping the latch and closing the front door behind him.

Through the traumas of the night he hadn't done much coherent thinking, but in the privacy of his empty early-morning railway compartment, he tried to bring an aching brain to bear on the subject.

The night before, his first thought was that Greg Marchmont must have been murdered. The sergeant knew too much and needed silencing. But morning reflection made him question this conclusion.

In some ways, for Marchmont to have been murdered didn't match the rest of the crime. Though he didn't hold much brief for most of what Roscoe had said, Charles agreed with the superintendent that the murderer was an exhibitionist, who got a charge from the way he was manipulating the police, the *Public Enemies* team, and indeed the entire British public.

Everything about the case so far showed meticulous planning skills. Though the crime was grotesque, its perpetrator had brilliantly controlled the flow of information about it, keeping always one step ahead of the official investigations, and providing dramatic climaxes for the weekly *Public Enemies* programmes with all the artistry of an award-winning screenwriter. His technique suggested someone familiar with the workings of police work or television – or, more likely, both.

Greg Marchmont fitted some elements of this profile, but there were others he didn't. For a start, he didn't appear to have enough intelligence or imagination to devise the killer's macabre scenario. Then again, his emotional tension and short temper seemed at odds with the cold-blooded detachment with which the crime must have been organized.

And, even though the faxes in his flat suggested the sergeant had been responsible for passing on information about the body parts to the police, Charles found it easier to cast him in a supporting role than as the initiator of the whole concept.

It seemed more credible that Greg Marchmont had sent the faxes on behalf of someone who had a hold over him.

That might explain his behaviour in Brighton too – clearing up the Trafalgar Lane flat on someone else's orders.

And it could also support the theory that his death was suicide. If Greg Marchmont had not only been responsible for sending the faxes, but also for arranging delivery of the gruesome package to the *Public Enemies* office – and the use of his chest and blanket suggested he was at least involved – then the pressure on him must have been intensifying beyond endurance.

The presence of the severed head in his flat – or maybe the instructions for what he had to do with it – might have proved too much. Stress on that scale could easily have pushed a man in his emotional state over into suicide – and the note he left could be interpreted to confirm such a supposition.

More important than all these arguments was the fact that Marchmont's suicide ruined the dramatic structure of the crime. The murderer's slight lapse, in making his first two discoveries of body parts too similar, had been more than retrieved by his stunning inspiration of the torso in the chest.

Surely the mastermind behind that must have planned some even more sensational *coup de théâtre* for the discovery of the head – particularly given the fact that it wasn't the head everyone was expecting.

But now that dramatic sequence had been broken. Presumably in the next few days Greg Marchmont's flat would be entered and the head in the pressure cooker found. And that discovery would be fed to the media in the usual journalistic way. Given the build-up, it would make a distinctly bathetic last act to the murderer's play.

For a moment, Charles toyed with the idea of the *Public Enemies* office receiving the suggestion that they take their cameras when the door to the flat was broken down. Bob Garston and Roger Parkes would have leapt at the idea, he was sure, and for Geoffrey Ramage, to direct the shot of the camera homing into the interior of the pressure cooker would have been the consummation of all his ambitions. To make the event even more exciting, they could do it as a live Outside Broadcast.

But, appealing though the idea might be to the programme-makers, Charles knew that even in television there are limits, and he couldn't see such a sequence being allowed by the IBA.

It would be another sensational first, though, for *Public*

Enemies – the entire ITV audience watching as the camera revealed that the severed head belonged not to Martin Earnshaw, but to Ted Faraday.

That change was the real shock, and Charles's battered mind had not yet worked out all the effects it had on his previous thinking about the case.

One immediate question arose – was there one murder victim or were there two? Did all the scattered body parts belong to Ted Faraday, or was it a kind of 'Mix'n'Match' situation between the dead private investigator and the dead property developer? The arms had certainly been identified as belonging to Martin Earnshaw. Which was why Charles Paris was once again travelling down to Brighton.

His first thought had been just to ring her up, but then he'd remembered that the police were recording all her calls, so decided on a face-to-face confrontation. The surveillance team might be recording everything that was said in the house as well, but that was a risk he'd have to take.

Even though it was daytime, there was still no one about in the road where Chloe Earnshaw lived. Before he rang the bell, Charles looked across, but no unmarked van was parked opposite. If the police protection was continuing, it now had a more discreet profile.

Chloe Earnshaw did not appear surprised by his arrival on her doorstep. Nor was she hostile. Indeed, she seemed pleased to see someone who had even the most tenuous connection with the world of television.

'I haven't had a single call from that *Public Enemies* lot for nearly a week,' she complained as she led Charles through into the kitchen. 'Tea? Coffee?'

'Coffee, please.' It might help his head a bit. 'You saw last night's programme, did you?'

'Yes.' She busied herself with the kettle.

'Must have been quite a shock for you.'

Chloe Earnshaw shrugged and turned to face him. She was swamped in a big black jumper that came down almost as far as her short black skirt. Tights and shoes were also black. 'Quite honestly, I've had so many shocks since this thing started, I hardly feel them any more.'

If she'd been saying that on camera, Charles reckoned, all over the country people would have been murmuring, 'Plucky little thing.' As before in Chloe's presence, he could feel the sexuality coming off her like a strong perfume. He had to remind himself how very unerotic actual physical contact in the form of their kiss had been.

'Still, if you did see the programme, you can understand why they didn't need you for any more reconstruction or appeals. A rather more dramatic development in the story had broken, hadn't it?'

'Yes, but they could have *told* me they weren't going to need me. I spent most of the week by the phone, waiting for them to call.'

Charles had heard those lines more times than he could recall, though usually from actresses who'd gone up to an interview for a television part and then not heard another word. He was struck by how very like a disgruntled actress Chloe Earnshaw behaved. Her husband's fate had become secondary to her own affront at being ignored by *Public Enemies*.

'They've obviously been very busy,' Charles conciliated, then couldn't help adding, 'and good manners are not something for which television as an industry is particularly well known.'

'Huh.' The kettle had boiled. Chloe Earnshaw turned back to make the coffee, continuing bitterly, 'I don't know – they pick you up, get you all excited, and then drop you – just like that.'

'Yes . . . When you say "get you all excited", you mean excited about the prospect of solving your husband's murder?'

Charles felt the reproachful beam of those dark blue eyes. 'Yes, of course I mean that.'

'Hmm . . . And have all the other telephone calls stopped too?'

'Which other telephone calls?'

'The ones from the members of the public.'

'Oh. Oh, those. There never were that many of those. I mean, the programme's phone lines got plenty, but hardly any came through here.'

'Except the one from the woman who'd seen Martin leaving the pub and going to the pier . . .'

'Oh, yes. Yes, of course, there was that one, but that's about it . . .'

'I thought you were moved back in here so that you could answer the phone if anyone rang . . . ?'

'That may have been one of the reasons. Sugar in your coffee?'

'No, just black. Thank you. Are the police still recording all your telephone calls?'

Another petulant shrug. 'I don't know. They're supposed to be. Mind you, they're *supposed* to be keeping me under twenty-four-hour surveillance and I haven't seen much sign of that recently either.'

'Well, they wouldn't want to make it obvious, would they?'

'If you're under surveillance by the British police, you *know* you're under surveillance by them. Look, they let you walk in here this morning without any questions, didn't they? You could have been a thug out to murder me for all anyone cares.'

'Mm. But have you actually been told by the police that they're stopping the surveillance?'

'I've been told they're "cutting it down". Some stuff about resources being stretched and personnel being needed for other duties. It seems I've ceased to be a priority with the police as

157

well as with *Public Enemies*.' The disgruntled actress tone in her voice was stronger than ever.

Charles thought about what she'd said. It could just be that the protection of Chloe Earnshaw had moved down the priorities, but, so long as the threat to her safety remained, that was unlikely. She had become such a nationally known figure, that if she came to any harm the police'd never live it down.

A more attractive thesis was that Chloe Earnshaw's protection had been scaled down because the risk to her was perceived to have diminished. Which could possibly suggest that the police knew that it wasn't her husband who had been murdered.

Time for Charles to move on to the reason for his visit. 'Chloe, do you ever consider the possibility that Martin might still be alive?'

It was a cue and Chloe Earnshaw took it like the professional she was. She went straight into television mode. The dark blue eyes misted over as the textbook answer came out. 'Well, of course I sometimes wake up in the morning thinking for a split second that it's all been a ghastly dream, but then reality comes thundering in. I kept thinking Martin was still alive for as long as I possibly could – even when every kind of logic told me how futile such hopes were. But once his arms were found, well . . . I couldn't pretend any more.'

There were plenty of Equity actresses Charles knew who couldn't have managed that little half-sob in the last few words.

'You identified the arms, didn't you?'

Chloe Earnshaw gave a brave little nod.

'Must've been ghastly for you.'

'Not the greatest moment of my life, no.'

'And . . . I hope you don't mind my asking this, but what about the other body parts?'

'*What* about them?'

'Did you have to go through the process of identifying them too?'

Chloe Earnshaw shook her head. 'I offered to, but it wasn't thought necessary. Once they'd checked that the various bits matched, that they came from the same body . . .' Her speech trickled away into quite convincing sobs. 'I think, if the head ever gets found, I'll have to . . .'

The picture she was building up seemed increasingly odd to Charles, though it did tie in with Sam Noakes's complaints about incomplete forensic examination. He wondered whether the scope of the police investigations into the case had been deliberately restricted.

'Could you . . . I'm sorry, Chloe, I know it must be painful for you to go back over all this, but I do have a reason for asking . . . could you tell me a bit more about when you identified the arms . . . ?'

She gulped, but gave a resolute little toss of her head. Charles may not have been a television audience of millions, but at least he was an audience. 'Yes, all right. What do you want to know?'

'I want to know how you actually did identify the arms as belonging to your husband.'

'Well, obviously they were his.'

'But how did you know? Was there any distinguishing mark you recognized? A mole? A scar?'

'No, nothing like that. I just *knew*.'

'So there was nothing that made you absolutely certain beyond any possible doubt that they belonged to him?'

'Well . . . There was his watch.'

'Ah.'

'It's a Rolex – well, it's not, it's a fake Rolex. One of Martin's clients brought it back from Hong Kong for him.'

'And that was still on the arm?'

'Yes.'

'Did you actually spend long looking at the arms?'

'No!' She grimaced. 'It's not something you want to spend long doing.'

'Of course not. So what exactly happened? Were the arms in a mortuary?'

'No, it was kind of a – I don't know, a forensic laboratory sort of place . . .'

'Here in Brighton?'

She nodded.

'And what . . . You went into the room and they were lying there on a table?'

'No, they were in a kind of drawer thing, and a woman police officer took me through to look at them.'

'What did she say to you?'

'She said, "There's something we'd like you to look at, Chloe, and I'm afraid it may be bad news." And I said, "What, you mean Martin?" and she said, "Yes, and I think I'd better tell you now – what you're going to see is two severed arms."'

'What did you say to that?'

'I said I felt sick. I *did*.'

'I'm not surprised.'

'And she said, "Don't worry, you won't have to look for long." And then I said I was OK, and she took me through and opened the drawer . . . and I could see the Rolex through the polythene and—'

'The arms were wrapped in polythene?'

'Yes. And I said, "That's him" and then I rushed out. I thought I was going to be sick.'

'Were you?'

'No, not as it happened, but she took me to the ladies' and I was crying and she . . .'

Chloe rambled on, but Charles was too preoccupied with his thoughts to listen much. It certainly didn't sound as if the identification of Martin Earnshaw's arms had been the most scientifically elaborate since forensic pathology began. The policewoman had put the thought into Chloe Earnshaw's mind of what she was about to see, and the confirmation of identity had been based on a momentary glimpse through polythene. It was only the fake Rolex that connected the limbs to Martin Earnshaw. And you can buy fake Rolexes all over the world.

If the arms has actually belonged to Ted Faraday, then it was likely that the rest of the body, as well as the head in the pressure cooker, was also Ted Faraday's.

Charles once more became aware of what Chloe was saying. ' ". . . but I'm going to see that whoever's done this awful crime is brought to justice. I don't care about my own safety, Sam," I said, "I just want—" '

'Sam? Did you say "Sam"?'

She nodded.

'You mean Sam Noakes? Sam Noakes was the woman police officer who accompanied you when you identified the arms?'

'Yes,' replied Chloe, puzzled by the urgency of his enquiry. 'But—'

He stopped. They looked at each other. Anxiety glinted in Chloe Earnshaw's eyes. They had both just heard the front door opened with a key.

Charles gave Chloe an interrogative look, and she nodded him permission – or something in fact more like an order – to go through into the hall.

Charles Paris pushed the kitchen door gently open.

A man with his anorak hood up stood in the hall. His back was to Charles as he closed the front door.

The man shook the hood off as he turned round.

It is hard to say which of them was the more surprised.

Charles Paris found himself looking at Martin Earnshaw.

Chapter Eighteen

Charles had been in this situation before, but only in Shakespeare plays.

He'd given his Sebastian in *Twelfth Night* at Norwich ('Sebastian is admittedly a boring part, but he doesn't need to be quite as boring as Charles Paris made him.' – *Eastern Evening News*), and when confronted by his cross-dressing twin Viola (played by a right little raver, as his memory served) had heard the Duke say:

> One face, one voice, one habit, and two persons;
> A natural perspective, that is, and is not.

Then again, in *A Comedy of Errors* at Exeter, he'd given his Antipholus of Syracuse ('Charles Paris twitched through the play, as if worried he might have left the gas on at home.' – *Western Morning News*) and, appearing on-stage for the first time with his unknown twin brother, Antipholus of Ephesus, had heard the duke (it's a rule in Shakepeare that only dukes get speeches like this) say:

> One of these men is Genius to the other;
> And so of these: which is the natural man,
> And which the spirit? Who deciphers them?

Facing Martin Earnshaw was different. For a start, Charles Paris didn't reckon they looked anything like each other. Mind you, he hadn't thought he looked much like the little raver playing Viola or the old queen playing Antipholus of Ephesus.

And in the Earnshaws' hall there was no handy duke ready with a little speech to convince everyone they looked alike – really. Charles was aware of Chloe moving to his shoulder.

Martin Earnshaw caught sight of his wife and a spasm, almost like fear, ran through him. 'Chloe,' he announced nervously, 'I had to come back and talk to you face to face.'

There was a hissing sound from behind Charles, as Chloe Earnshaw, the nation's favourite tragic widow, spat out the words, 'You bastard! I told you never to dare come back here!'

Suddenly she was past Charles and into the hall, hurling herself at her husband. Martin Earnshaw raised arms to shield his face as her nails ripped towards it. He backed away from her flying feet as they hacked into his shins.

Charles was so surprised that it took a moment before he moved in to get Chloe off her husband. By then she had pulled a horn-handled walking-stick out of the hall-stand and was about to bring it down on Martin Earnshaw's head.

She was amazingly strong and, as Charles pinioned her arms, turned all her aggression on him. He felt the nails gouge into the flesh beneath his eye and the teeth meet through his sports jacket and forearm. It took a full five minutes before he could subdue her.

'It's not something any man's proud to admit,' said Martin Earnshaw, 'that his wife beats up on him.'

'No,' Charles Paris agreed, feeling the bruises on his face swelling.

'A battered husband – I mean, it just sounds so pathetic.'

Each had a pint of beer. They were sitting in the pub in Trafalgar Lane into which Charles had followed Greg Marchmont only a few weeks before. They were there because it was near the station and Martin had arranged to meet someone who was arriving on a train from London.

'Has she been like that ever since you've known her?'

163

'No, obviously not right at the start. I'd never have married her if I'd seen her in one of those moods. But really, from the moment we were married – even on the honeymoon – she started hitting me.'

'And you never hit her back?'

'No, I'm . . . I've never really been that kind of person. I was a bit naive, I suppose. My first marriage worked fine, but unfortunately my wife died. I met Chloe and, well . . . I was very flattered that someone as young and dishy as her was interested in me. She was the one who suggested getting married, actually. I'd never have dared ask her, but . . . well, I couldn't believe my luck, and I just assumed that everything would be like it was with my first wife. I certainly wasn't left with that illusion for long.' He took a rueful sip of beer.

'Didn't you think about just leaving her, walking out?'

'Oh, of course I did, but it wasn't easy. It takes a long time to believe something like that's actually happening to you. You think things'll change, get better.'

'But they didn't?'

A gloomy shake of the head. 'No. I did make elaborate plans for escape when I first realized what the situation was. I thought of going abroad. I even took to carrying my passport around with me all the time. But somehow . . . being with Chloe sort of sapped my will. I couldn't . . . I don't know . . .'

He shuddered. 'Then there were financial reasons why I had to stay. I'd got a lot of money tied up in the house. I worked from there, apart from anything else. If things'd been better, I could maybe have afforded to get out, but . . . well, you probably know the property market hasn't been at its brilliant best the last few years.'

'I did just hear about that, yes.'

'And . . . well . . .' Martin Earnshaw looked embarrassed. 'The fact is, I'm not the most dynamic person that was ever created. I admit that. With my first wife it didn't matter – she loved me, she gave me confidence, and we had lots of friends, we were fine. I just didn't know how to cope with someone like Chloe. She isolated us as a couple ... one by one, stopped me seeing all my friends, everyone I'd known before I met her. It got horribly claustrophobic. Also I can't pretend – I was absolutely terrified of her. And even though she spent all her time criticizing and getting at me, I don't think she wanted me to leave her. I think she wanted me to stay around ...'

'As a punchbag, you mean?'

He grinned ruefully. Charles noticed a matching bruise to his own was swelling beneath Martin Earnshaw's eye. 'Pretty much, yes. And of course working at home made it all worse. I was around all the time, and the work was going badly, and the money was running out.'

'Did you borrow to cover your debts?'

'As much as I could, yes. But that wasn't much. Not a bank's favourite kind of customer – an unsuccessful property developer paying out huge mortgages on properties nobody wants to buy.'

'So did you try anywhere else?'

'What do you mean?'

'Anywhere other than the bank?'

Martin Earnshaw looked genuinely puzzled. '*Is* there anywhere other than the bank?'

'Have you heard of loan sharks?'

'Well, I've heard of them, from the press, television documentaries and so on, but I've never met one.'

Charles began to realize the scale on which Chloe Earnshaw had built up her huge edifice of lies. And he also realized how almost every detail of the case had come from her testimony.

It was Chloe Earnshaw who had reported her husband missing. It was Chloe Earnshaw who had said he'd got involved with loan sharks. She had also provided background by telling how he'd arrived home beaten up a few weeks before his disappearance – though, given her propensity for violence, he might well have been seen around with a few bruises.

Charles had a sudden thought. 'Did you have any life insurance?'

'Yes, I did, actually, a couple of quite decent policies. When things got bad, I suggested we should cash them in, but Chloe said no. She said, as my wife, she ought to get some money if anything happened to me.'

Or if the entire country could be convinced that something had happened to you, thought Charles. He could see another reason why Chloe Earnshaw might have been so ready to identify the severed arms as those of her husband.

'How was it that you finally did come to leave her?'

'I don't know. I just snapped. She'd beaten up on me really bad one Sunday evening. I think she'd broken a couple of ribs – hurt like hell.' He rubbed a hand gingerly across his front. 'Still does. And, anyway, I thought, if I let this go on, one day she's going to kill me. So I just said I was going.'

'And what effect did that have?'

'She got hold of a broom handle and went for me even harder. And she was shouting all this stuff – that if I went, I'd never be able to come back – she'd kill me if she ever saw me again. It was terrifying. I thought she'd kill me if I stayed, and all, so I just left – out the front door, gone.'

'And then you went to the pub?'

Martin Earnshaw looked bewildered. 'Went to the pub? What do you mean?'

'The Black Feathers. The pub down in the Lanes.'

'I've never been to a pub in the Lanes in my life.'

'Oh.'

So all the painstaking filming for *Public Enemies* had been reconstructing something that never happened. The sighting of Martin Earnshaw in the pub had just been another of Chloe Earnshaw's fabrications. Charles remembered vaguely that the

details were supposed to have been telephoned to her anony-
mously. Easy enough to make that up.

The subsequent call – from the woman who claimed to have
seen Martin Earnshaw walking from the pub to the pier – must
have been more difficult to engineer, because by then the police
had a bug on the Earnshaw's telephone. Still, not impossible.
It had been recorded on the answering machine while Chloe was
out shopping, and the voice had sounded as if it was disguised.

The police, who seemed as caught up in the glamour of
television as anyone, might not have investigated such a call too
closely. So long as it provided some more action for *Public
Enemies* to reconstruct, everyone was happy.

'So, Martin, where did you go when you left the house?'

'I just walked. I didn't know where I was going. I was so
relieved to be out of there. I just walked. And then, when I kind
of came to, I realized I was walking east, out of Brighton, and
I thought, that's the way to Newhaven. So I walked on and I'd
got a bit of cash on me – still carrying my passport too – so I
caught the late-night ferry to Dieppe. And I've been in France
ever since.'

'So you don't know what's been going on here?'

'What do you mean?'

'About your disappearance.'

He chuckled. 'Nobody's interested in whether I've disappeared or not.'

Don't you believe it, thought Charles. One day you really
must see the audience figures for *Public Enemies* over the last
few weeks. But he let it pass, for the time being.

'The obvious question, though, Martin, is – why have you
come back now?'

'Ah. Well, you see . . .' A rather charming coyness came over
him. 'In France I met this girl . . . woman, really. In Dieppe.
First day – it must have been meant. I was having a coffee with,
like, virtually the last money I had, and she was the waitress,

167

and we got talking and . . . well, the upshot was . . . her father'd just died and her mother was having difficulty coping with the farm they'd got . . . and so, last few weeks, I've just been helping out . . .'

'Ah.' If Martin Earnshaw'd been hidden away on a French farm, it would explain why no television-watching English tourists had spotted him.

He gave another coy smile. 'And the fact is . . . Veronique, that's this girl – well, woman . . . she and I . . . well, we've become very close. We're going to live together.'

'Oh?'

'She's lovely, she really is. But I thought, I can't just set up with someone else, I've got to *tell* Chloe . . . you know, to her face, actually have a confrontation, tell her what's what.'

'Brave thing to do, in the circumstances.'

'Yes. I wouldn't have dared if I hadn't met Veronique. She's given me confidence. Otherwise I'd never have gone near Chloe again – under any circumstances.'

Charles began to realize how safe Chloe Earnshaw had been in her fabrications about her husband's death. She'd got Martin so terrified, he'd have done anything rather than have to face her again. It was only his meeting Veronique that had thrown Chloe's plans. Without a new woman in his life, he'd never have posed any threat to his wife's machinery of self-publicity.

'So you came to Brighton this morning to have the confrontation?'

Martin Earnshaw nodded. 'Yes, Veronique's gone up to London to do some shopping. She thought I was daft, but I said seeing Chloe was something that had to be done.'

'A man's gotta do what a man's gotta do,' Charles rumbled in suitable American.

'Yes.'

'And do you still feel that?'

A quick shake of the head. 'No. Don't know why I ever did.

168

And the great thing is, Veronique won't mind whether I have done or whether I haven't.' He was almost crowing with happiness. 'She is great, you know. Seeing Chloe again made me realize just how great. And how awful things were. When I was in the same room with Chloe this morning, I just felt all my will drain out of me. I couldn't do anything. If you hadn't been there, I'd never have got away from her again.'

Charles Paris grinned. 'Glad to have been of service. Another pint?'

At that moment two people entered the pub. As Charles moved to the bar, he saw a solidly attractive dark-haired woman come in, not together with, but at the same time as, an elderly man.

The woman, from the way Martin Earnshaw hurried to greet her, had to be Veronique. And she looked as nice and warm as he said she was.

The elderly man was Kevin Littlejohn.

He looked at Charles Paris and froze. Then he turned towards the bar and saw Martin Earnshaw.

Kevin Littlejohn did a classic double-take, and fainted.

The two men hurried forward to help.

'What on earth's the matter with him?' asked Martin Earnshaw.

'He just thinks we look alike.'

'You and me?' Martin looked sceptically into Charles's face. 'But we don't look anything like each other, do we?'

'No,' said Charles Paris on a bit of a giggle. 'No, we don't.'

Chapter Nineteen

It was daft, he knew, given the fact that there was only a pay-phone there, but he preferred to make his calls from Hereford Road. Or maybe homing back in on where he lived – however unwelcoming it might be – gave him a feeling of continuity, or even of security.

He was back home by four o'clock. Having stiffened the odd sinew with a slurp of Bell's, he got out the paper on which he'd scribbled the numbers from Louise Denning's index, and went to the payphone on the landing.

Stuck to the wall was a message on a yellow sticker. Must have been written by one of the Junoesque – or perhaps Frank Brunoesque – Swedish girls who inhabited the other bedsitters.

'CHARLES PARRISH – JULIET RINGED.'

His first thought was 'Who on earth do I know called Juliet?', before, with shame, he realized it was his daughter. They hadn't spoken for months. Get the difficult call out of the way first, thought Charles, then I'll phone Juliet. Though he had a guilty feeling that the second might not be a particularly easy call either.

He rang Sam Noakes's office number and got through straight away. Her voice was deterrently professional. 'Yes, who is it?'

'Charles Paris.'

'Who? Oh, you're the actor in the reconstructions.' Her voice took on a more forbidding you're-not-going-to-waste-my-time-again-are-you tone. 'What do you want?'

'I've got some more information. On the Martin Earnshaw case.'

'All right. Tell me about it.'

'I think it'd be better if we met.'

She didn't think that was at all a good idea.

'It concerns Ted Faraday. And Greg Marchmont. It's quite sensational stuff.'

She was clearly tempted, but asked, 'What makes you think it's information we haven't already got?'

'I haven't seen anything in the media about it. And once this breaks, even you are going to have difficulty keeping it quiet.'

She decided quickly. 'All right. Come and see me at my office.'

Sam Noakes wasn't actually based in Scotland Yard, but in a nearby Victorian building, which showed signs of recent and incomplete conversion into offices.

'Only just moved in here,' she explained when she met him from the lift. 'We were spilling out of the main building. Ours is one of the fastest growing departments.'

'What department is that?'

'It's officially called "Television and Media Liaison". But we're known throughout the force as the "Video Nasties".'

'Oh.'

In the corridor they passed uniformed men and women, who all acknowledged the inspector with the same respect Charles had noticed from her colleagues in the WET hospitality suite.

'Is Superintendent Roscoe based here too?' he asked.

Sam Noakes grimaced. 'Yes, for about another week. He's extended his retirement till after the end of the *Public Enemies* series. *Then* maybe we'll be able to get some proper work done round here. Come through.'

The inspector led him into a small office sliced off by unpainted chipboard partitions and gestured to a minimally upholstered chair. She sat with her back to the window behind a commendably tidy desk. Her striped shirt and jeans expressed that casualness which takes great care and money.

'And who takes over from Roscoe when he goes?'

'There another old fart sitting in for a few months – but at least he's one who won't interfere so much. Then they'll promote someone permanent. The role of the department's changing so quickly at the moment that they don't want to rush into an appointment.'

'Is it likely to go to someone already working here?'

Sam Noakes gave an enigmatic shrug that didn't rule out the possibility of her being in the running for the job.

Then she straightened up and became businesslike. 'Right, tell me what you've got. It'd better be good.'

'It is,' said Charles Paris. 'Have you heard anything from Sergeant Marchmont in the last few days?'

She shook her head dismissively. 'He's on sick leave. He's got nothing to do with the case now.'

Her unconcern sounded genuine. It was hard to believe that she did know anything about the contents of Marchmont's flat. But then, if some of Charles's suspicions of her were correct, Sam Noakes was highly skilled in deceit.

'What about Ted Faraday? Have you heard anything from him?'

'There've been a few faxes from Brighton – apparently he's still working undercover. *Claims* to be making progress with the investigation, but I've seen no evidence of it so far.'

Again her ignorance of the private investigator's true fate sounded sincere. Again Charles had to remind himself of the deviousness of the criminal he was up against. Somebody had killed Faraday and maintained the myth of his continued existence by faxing reports from him. Or rather by making Greg Marchmont fax reports from him. So the criminal was someone with a hold over the sergeant. By that criterion, Sam Noakes definitely qualified as a suspect.

'Inspector, when Chloe Earnshaw identified the arms as her husband's, I believe you were with her . . . ?'

'Yes, I was.' Noakes seemed suddenly to realize that she was losing control of the conversation. 'Mr Paris, I invited you here because you said you had some information on the case, not so that you could start interrogating me.'

'It's relevant.'

'Bloody well better be.' She sank back into her chair and sulkily allowed him to continue.

'From what Chloe Earnshaw's told me, it seems that her inspection of the severed arms was extremely perfunctory.'

'It's not something you want to bloody linger over. The poor girl had been through hell since her husband disappeared, fearing the worst. Now suddenly the worst had happened. I wasn't about to put her through another major ordeal. The identification was only a formality.'

'Why? Didn't the possibility ever occur to you that the arms might have belonged to someone else?'

'Oh, come *on*. They were found near Brighton. Their owner seemed to have been killed round the time Martin Earnshaw disappeared. The arms belonged to someone the right size, the right age.'

Yes, thought Charles. My size, my age. He remembered how in the hospitality suite Greg Marchmont had mistaken him for Ted Faraday. Faraday, Martin Earnshaw and Charles Paris were all about the same size and the same age.

'And presumably more would be found out about the arms by more detailed forensic examination?'

'Presumably.'

'But you implied when we spoke before, that more detailed forensic examination never took place.'

Sam Noakes looked truculent. 'It was deferred. Until the whole body had been found.'

'The police have great advantages, don't they, in organizing how a case is pursued?'

'Of course we do. That's our job.'

173

'But, if a policeman – or woman, with privileged information, wanted to control the direction of enquiries . . . by, say, ensuring that the forensic investigation was inadequate, it wouldn't be difficult to do, would it?'

'Perhaps not. But why would they *want* to do it?'

Charles shrugged. 'Any number of reasons . . . To make their own role in the proceedings look more important than it actually was . . . ? To impress a television audience . . . ?'

'What are you actually saying, Mr Paris?'

'I'm just thinking round the case. Asking, really, whether, when you were with Chloe Earnshaw looking at the severed arms, it ever occurred to you for a moment that they might belong to someone other than her husband?'

'Of course not. Look, the investigation was under way. We'd got the public's interest through *Public Enemies* – finding those arms was just the breakthrough we needed.' The pale blue eyes sparkled as she became caught up in the excitement of recollection. 'And the way we broke the story on that week's programme . . . now that was really something.'

It could have been Bob Garston or Roger Parkes speaking. Charles realized just how much her instincts as a member of the police force had been swamped by the values of television.

'So . . .' he hazarded gently, 'if Chloe Earnshaw hadn't identified the arms as belonging to her husband . . . ?'

'Well, it would have screwed up bloody everything, wouldn't it!' Sam Noakes realized this was a bit indiscreet and hastened to cover up. 'Anyway, she identified him from his watch.'

'A fake Rolex? Plenty of those about. And presumably you had descriptions of all the stuff he was wearing when he disappeared?'

'Of course we did.' A hard, resentful light came into the pale blue eyes. 'Mr Paris, what are you suggesting?'

'Just that if someone in the police force wanted Chloe Earnshaw to identify those limbs as her husband's, it wouldn't have been very difficult to fix it so that she did.'

'But they *were* her husband's! Nobody needed to fix anything. And I may tell you, Mr Paris, that the kind of allegations you seem to be making against the police are not—'

'The arms don't belong to Martin Earnshaw,' said Charles Paris calmly.

'*What!*'

'I spent lunchtime today in a Brighton pub, drinking beer with Martin Earnshaw.'

This revelation completely winded her. The inspector gaped at Charles, incapable of speech. He took advantage of the silence to press on. 'I also know what's happened to Greg Marchmont and Ted Faraday. I'm afraid it's not good news in either case.'

'What do you mean – what's happened to them?'

'I know they were both your lovers.'

'So bloody what!' Her eyes blazed. 'I'd like to know what my private life has to do with you.'

'Greg would have done anything for you, anything you asked . . .'

'So . . .'

'Did you ever ask him to do anything . . . ?'

'Like what?'

'Anything illegal?'

'No! Listen, Greg and I lived together for a while, but it didn't work out – end of story.'

'Then you joined up with Ted Faraday.'

'So? What business is that of yours?'

'And is that relationship still going on?'

She smiled now, a superior smile of sexual confidence. 'We still see each other from time to time. We're both grown-ups, you know. We see other people and when work and what-have-you permits, maybe we'll spend the odd night together. There are other friends with whom I have similar relationships.'

'Is Bob Garston one of them?'

She gave him a feline smile. The attraction of boasting about her sexual power overcame her instinct for discretion. 'You don't have to be a man to have control over your own sex life, you know.'

Her mood changed. She realized how much she was allowing herself to be sidetracked by vanity. 'Come on, you said you had some information. If you have, tell it to me. Otherwise, get the hell out of here!'

'One more piece of information I want you to tell me, then I'll tell you mine.'

'What?' she asked sullenly.

'Greg Marchmont nearly got kicked out of the force a little while back, didn't he?'

'Yes.'

'For being drunk on duty?'

'That's right. He'd really gone to pieces over the last year.' She gave Charles a stubborn look, daring him to make any accusations. 'And it wasn't my bloody fault. If he couldn't cope with us splitting up, then that was his problem, not mine. I needed to move on.'

Story of your life, thought Charles. You'll always need to move on. And up. And if a few Greg Marchmonts get washed up in your wake . . . well, that's just their bad luck.

But all he said was, 'So why wasn't Greg Marchmont kicked out?'

She shrugged. 'I don't know. It was odd. He seemed all set to get the boot, then suddenly he was staying on. Guess someone interceded for him. Must have a friend in high places.'

Yes, thought Charles Paris, he must.

He looked across at Sam Noakes and thought again how beautiful she was. How beautiful and how completely heartless. And he replied to the insistent enquiry in her pale blue eyes.

'The solution to this case – or at least part of the solution to this case – is in Greg Marchmont's flat. You'd better send someone over there right away.'

'But is Greg all right?' she asked, suddenly anxious.

'No,' said Charles Paris. 'He's dead. And so, I'm afraid, is Ted Faraday.'

The news caught her like a slap in the face. Moisture gathered in her eyes.

In the brief instant before she regained control, Detective Inspector Sam Noakes looked human.

Chapter Twenty

Charles told her more about what to expect in the flat, but Sam Noakes's brief moment of vulnerability was past. The fact that both dead men had been her lovers had become irrelevant. She appeared to have no problem stomaching the most gruesome details.

'You should have reported this immediately you found it,' she reproved him. 'You have a duty to—'

'I think there have been duties inadequately fulfilled on both sides,' said Charles evenly.

She held his gaze with defiance, but after a moment looked away and let it pass. 'You say you think Sergeant Marchmont's death was suicide?'

'Looks that way to me. It also makes more sense in the logic of the whole case that he did it himself.'

'Would you care to expand on that?'

Charles Paris shook his head. 'I'm sure the last thing you want at this point in your investigation is to hear the theories of an amateur.'

With a little nod of her head, she acknowledged the point scored. 'So you have no idea who committed the original murder, Mr Paris?'

He shrugged deferentially. 'I always leave that stuff to the police, Inspector.'

She picked up a phone on her desk. 'I'm sure you can find your way back to the lift.' Charles rose and she ignored him as he walked to the door of her office. 'Hello, Noakes here,' she barked into the telephone. 'I need a car – like fast!'

Charles made his way slowly to the lift, knowing he had no

178

intention of leaving the building yet. He asked a uniformed policewoman for directions.

There was no one in the outer office. A typewriter shrouded by a dusty cover suggested there hadn't been a secretary there for some time. Compared to the bustle of the rest of the building, the area was very still. It wasn't where the department's action happened.

Charles Paris knocked on the inner door, and a startled voice told him to come in.

Superintendent Roscoe was sitting by the window, and the movement of his swivel-chair suggested he'd been looking out of it before Charles's arrival. The office he occupied was large and might in time be luxurious, but the decorations were half done. There seemed to be no air of urgency about finishing them. The superintendent would be gone in a couple of weeks, after all. No point in making an effort for someone just working out his time.

Roscoe recognized Charles immediately, and seemed pleased to see him. The intrusion of anyone into his solitude was welcome.

He gestured to a seat. 'So to what do I owe this pleasure, Mr Paris? You haven't been doing your own amateur investigations again, have you?'

'I have found out a few odd things, yes. Been talking to Greg Marchmont.'

'Ah, poor Marchmont. He's been off sick for the last few days. Pressure was getting to him a bit.'

'I'm not surprised.'

'What do you mean by that?' Roscoe asked sharply.

But Charles Paris wasn't quite ready to go into the attack. 'I just meant that it's a stressful job, being a policeman, isn't it?'

'Yes. You have to be pretty tough to get through.'

'But you have, Superintendent – got through – all the way through to retirement.'

'Nearly.'

'Which is something Greg Marchmont won't do.'

'I don't see why not.'

The reaction was so instinctive that Charles now knew Marchmont's death had been suicide. The Sergeant couldn't cope any more with the pressure that had been put on him. But, even as he shot himself, he must have known that his death would also destroy the person who had imposed that pressure.

'Greg Marchmont won't make retirement, Superintendent,' said Charles in a level voice, 'because he's dead.'

'What?'

'He didn't mind sending anonymous faxes about the where-abouts of the body parts. He even coped with cleaning up the flat in Trafalgar Lane . . . where you had butchered Ted Fara-day. He wasn't keen on arranging the packaging and delivery of the torso, but he did it. The head, though . . . the head was too much.'

Superintendent Roscoe was staring at him with horrified fas-cination. 'Marchmont isn't really dead,' he murmured. 'He can't be. It'd ruin everything.'

'I'm afraid everything is ruined already. So, unless you tell someone, we'll never know how you were intending to spring the revelation of the head on to the great British public.'

There was a sudden movement as Roscoe reached to one of his desk drawers. Charles found himself looking down the barrel of an automatic pistol, very like the one that had killed Marchmont.

'I could still make the arrangements myself. I can get rid of you, Mr Paris, with no problem, and if you're the only person who knows about Marchmont's death, then—'

'Ah, but I'm not.' Charles sounded considerably more laid back than he felt. 'No, I'm afraid Sam Noakes is on her way to Marchmont's flat – even as we speak.'

A spasm of anger crossed the superintendent's face and the

gun wavered dangerously in his hand. Then, listlessly, he dropped it on to the desk. 'If I don't get to the payoff, to the final act of the drama, then the whole thing's been a waste of time.'

'Why did you do it, though, Superintendent?'

'To prove that I could.' A spark of energy glinted in his eye. 'To show all those smug young bastards that I could run circles round them. You may imagine I don't know how they think of me, but I do. Boring, incompetent old Roscoe. He can do bugger all as a policeman and won't it be a bloody relief for everyone when he finally retires. But I showed them. By God, I showed them! They all agreed that they were up against a criminal with a brilliant mind, but they didn't know just how brilliant.'

As he spoke, the glee of his self-regard mingled with the bitterness of an entire career spent without respect or affection from any of his colleagues.

'And, of course, it enabled you to get rid of Ted Faraday.'

'Yes.' Roscoe nodded with relish. 'The smuggest of all the young bastards. Thought he knew it all, thought he could do it all, thought he could mix with crooks and get away with it . . . kept saying he "understood the criminal mind". Well, he didn't understand *my* criminal mind. You should have seen the expression in his eyes when he realized I'd got him, when he realized I was going to kill him. That made the whole bloody thing worthwhile.'

'You killed him in Brighton?'

'In the flat, yes. Made him suffer for an hour or two, after I'd told him I was going to do it. Then I strangled him.' The superintendent let out a little giggle at the recollection. 'Beautiful job, sweet as a nut.'

'And you planned the whole *Public Enemies* thing, feeding the bits of the body to them.'

'Yes . . .' Roscoe nodded proudly. 'It's my job, after all. "Television and Media Liaison". The job they all said I couldn't

181

do. But I bloody showed them. Produced the best set of "Video Nasties" ever.'

'And you *intended* that everyone should think the body was Martin Earnshaw?'

'Oh yes, you bet. And it was wonderful how willing everyone was to believe it. Those two tarts – Chloe Earnshaw and our brilliant little sexpot Sam Noakes – oh, they lapped it up. I only had to plant the idea in their heads and they were away, like a pair of bitches on heat. Anything to ensure they got another appearance on precious bloody television. Bob Garston and the *Public Enemies* lot were just as easy to convince. They didn't give a shit about the truth, so long as they got something to make the public switch on. It's amazing how easy it is to make people believe what they want to believe.'

'And meanwhile you controlled the investigation – stopped it going into too much depth when you didn't want it to, limited the amount of forensic examination, all that?'

'Yes, I'd do that and they'd all say, "Bloody Roscoe – always putting the dampers on everything – boring old fart – God, he's so thick." And all the time I was making them dance to my tune like a bunch of bloody puppets.'

He chuckled again at his own remembered cleverness. 'And I kept saying things to them, like "I've a feeling you're very close to this murderer", stuff like that . . . and they never bloody knew how right I was!'

'When we were going down to Brighton, you told me the criminal was an exhibitionist.'

'Exactly! I remember. And I told you that the case was going to be the triumph of my career. And . . .' He giggled on the edge of hysteria '. . . oh, I was sailing close to the wind then. Do you remember what I had in the boot of the car that day?'

'Well, I . . . Your golf clubs.'

'I've never played golf in my life.'

'But . . . So what was in . . . ? Oh my God,' said Charles, as he realized the implication. 'The legs?'

Superintendent Roscoe grinned complacently. 'Yes, I bought the golf bag in Brighton. I put the legs in and took them up to London and back again – in a bloody police car, for God's sake – just for the fun of doing it!'

'And it was you in disguise who I followed when you were going to plant the legs in the station car park?'

Roscoe looked at him in surprise. 'Yes, that was me. I was really sailing close to the wind then – I enjoyed that. And then when you were banged up down in Brighton, you told me all about it . . . and I could hardly stop myself from telling you it was me you'd been following.'

'But most of the dirty work you got Marchmont to do for you?'

'Mm. He was only still in the force on my say-so, and his life was so fucked up the job was about the only thing he had left. I knew he'd do anything I told him, anything. And once he'd started, he was implicated. An accessory to murder – no way he was going to blab about it then.'

'Except he couldn't stand the pressure.'

'No. The stupid bugger!' Roscoe slammed his fist on the desk in frustration. 'He's screwed up the whole bloody thing!'

'But if he hadn't . . . ? If you'd managed your final coup – and got the discovery of the head announced on *Public Enemies* – what then?'

The superintendent sighed. 'I hadn't really thought that far. Just do it, round off the whole perfect sequence – that was all I'd thought about. Oh, I don't know, I might have staged a neat little suicide for Marchmont *after* the end of the series. There was enough evidence pointing in his direction for everyone to think he'd done the lot. I could have fixed that, but . . .' His eyes grew distant and unfocused. 'I hadn't really thought beyond finishing it . . . my final triumph. Retirement?' He screwed up his face. 'I don't think I'd be much good at retirement. Being in the police's been my life. Maybe I never was much good at it, but it was my life . . .'

Charles brought the superintendent out of his reverie by asking, 'And what had you got in mind for the final *Public Enemies*? How were you going to stage the revelation of the head?'

'Well, I was . . .' Roscoe stopped, and a sly smile came to his lips. 'I'm not going to tell you. We all have our professional secrets, after all.'

'Ah. Right. And now . . . ?'

'Now?' The superintendent spoke as if he didn't understand the word.

'Yes, what are you going to do now?'

'Oh.' He looked bleakly out of the window. 'I hadn't really thought.'

'I mean, there's no way your involvement can be kept quiet now. I don't mean that I'm going to say anything, but I'm pretty sure Noakes and her lot will start to put two and two together. Once it's known that the murder victim's Ted Faraday and not Martin Earnshaw . . .'

'Yes, yes . . . Oh, I'm sure they'll work it out. They may not be quite in my class, but they're not stupid.' Superintendent Roscoe sounded bored now, as if he were speaking of something which didn't involve him at any level.

'Well . . .' Charles shrugged. 'I guess how you play that is up to you.'

'Hm.' Roscoe nodded abstractedly. 'Yes, I guess it is.'

He was silent, locked away in his own thoughts.

Charles Paris rose from his chair. Just before he got to the door, he looked back, but the murderer was miles away, in a world of his own.

It was while he was waiting for the lift that Charles Paris heard the muffled crack of a gunshot.

Chapter Twenty-One

He took in a few pubs and an Italian restaurant on the way back, so it was nearly midnight when he finally reached Hereford Road. As he walked past the payphone, he remembered that he'd never rung Juliet, and his shame was increased by the sight of another sticker, bearing the message: 'CARL PARRIS – PLEESE RING JULIETTE.'

It'd have to wait till the morning. Juliet might not have minded a call at that hour, but her husband Miles, insurance maestro and heavily backed favourite in the Most Boring Man In Britain Stakes, certainly would.

It wasn't a good night. Charles's thoughts churned blackly and his brief moments of sleep were crowded with images of dismembered daughters. Drinking more Bell's to try and shift the mood probably didn't help either.

He waited till half past eight to ring Juliet. 'It's me, Charles.'

'Oh, Daddy, I've been trying to contact you for days.'

'Yes, well, I've, er, sort of been . . . you know.'

'I just didn't know if you knew about Mummy . . .'

'Knew what about Mummy?'

'She's in hospital.'

'Hospital? Why?'

'Oh, just for some tests.'

Frances looked very pale and thin with her dark – now dyed dark – hair spread out over the pillow. But she managed a grin when she saw who had come to visit.

'Charles, you shouldn't have bothered. I'm not going to be in here long.'

'But I . . . I couldn't not have come to see you.'

She didn't look totally convinced by this.

He sat down at the bedside. 'I haven't brought you anything, I'm afraid. You know, grapes or . . .'

'I'll survive.'

He desperately wanted to ask her why she was there, what was wrong, but somehow the words wouldn't form themselves into the right order.

He took her hand. She didn't resist. He fondled it in his, feeling the reassuring ridge of the kitchen knife scar on her thumb, and was swamped by the knowledge of how much she meant to him.

Frances's hand returned the pressure. He kissed her thin lips.

The last episode of *Public Enemies* was, inevitably, an anticlimax. The news media were not going to let themselves be upstaged again and were hungry for revenge.

The story broke on the Saturday, so the weekend papers and television news bulletins took great pleasure in producing ever new revelations about the death and dismemberment of Ted Faraday. All their reports made references to *Public Enemies*, the television programme which had devoted nearly a whole series to investigating the wrong murder.

By the following Thursday the public was sick to death of the story and of the very mention of *Public Enemies*. They voted with their feet – or rather with their remote controls – and the ITV ratings plummeted. *Dad's Army* had never been so popular.

Bob Garston and Bob's Your Uncle Productions, realizing that the prospects for another series of *Public Enemies* had been seriously jeopardized, started developing a new True Crime format called *The Sex Offenders*. This would reconstruct historic and current sex crimes with the same public-spirited grittiness which had characterized *Public Enemies*. The thinking was that an appeal to the public's prurient fascination with sex, as well as to their prurient fascination with violence, could not fail.

Bob's Your Uncle Productions did not mention the new idea to Roger Parkes, whose contract at WET had not been renewed. Geoffrey Ramage, however, thought he was in with a chance of being employed because in his time he'd directed quite a few blue movies.

The Sex Offenders, however, fell foul of an increasingly puritanical IBA, and was abandoned at an advanced stage of preparation, after Bob's Your Uncle Productions had spent a considerable amount of development money.

Bob Garston, so recently flavour of the month, suddenly couldn't be given away with soap. His girlfriend, Detective Inspector Sam Noakes, very quickly left the sinking ship and started an affair with a junior cabinet minister who was very strong on law and order issues.

Her police career continued to advance, but not as quickly as had once been prophesied. When the new head of the 'Video Nasties' department was announced, it wasn't Sam Noakes. Her involvement in the *Public Enemies* debacle had left a permanent black mark against her.

The true story of Ted Faraday's death never emerged. The police closed ranks and, though the suicides of Greg Marchmont and Superintendent Roscoe were reported, no connection was ever made between them and the private investigator's murder.

So far as the public knew – and it was a thought which gave them a deliciously unpleasant *frisson* – the man who had killed and dismembered Ted Faraday was 'still at large'.

Chloe Earnshaw was not prosecuted for wasting police time. Though her fabrications had cost them hundreds of thousands, it was reckoned impossible to proceed against her without raising embarrassing questions about the force's own shortcomings during the investigation.

Martin Earnshaw became a kind of folk hero. His simple manner and the tag of 'The Man Who Came Back From The

Dead' made him ideal tabloid fodder. And when he married his beloved Veronique, the paparazzi gave the occasion almost as much coverage as a royal divorce. The couple retired happily to her family farm, where they bred Limousin cattle and children.

Chloe Earnshaw, almost as discredited as Bob Garston but still drawn to publicity like a moth to flame, tried to set up a charitable trust to help victims of tabloid character assassination. She arranged a major launch, featuring a couple of minor film actors, three rock musicians, a television weather girl and innumerable soap stars.

Unfortunately, though the event was well organized and publicized, no press arrived to cover it. Chloe Earnshaw should have realized that she would never get away with biting the hand that had so lavishly fed her.

Within a year, the public had completely forgotten the name of Chloe Earnshaw. And that hurt more than any of the supposed sufferings during her brief camera-flash of fame.

The tests on Frances were inconclusive. 'There's nothing to worry about,' said the consultant jovially, 'or if there is we haven't found it!'

She said she felt fine, but still tired easily. Her husband made all kinds of extravagant promises that he'd keep more closely in touch with her, that he'd really try to rebuild their relationship.

But Charles Paris remained Charles Paris, and the road to hell is paved with empty bottles of Bell's.

He went back into empty-glove-puppet mode, and his so-called 'career' returned to its customary stasis. The theatre was, as Maurice Skellern put it, 'very quiet', and nobody seemed to be making television drama any more. Or those who did seemed determined not to employ Charles Paris in their productions.

Sometimes, when things were really bad, Charles would walk through the streets of London and, if he saw someone of approximately his build and age, would think idly to himself, 'If

I killed that man, I might be employed to play him in a television reconstruction of the murder. But is it really worth the hassle?'

Generally speaking, the answer he came up with was no.